D1290274

FOOL'S GOLD

By Patty Wyatt Slack

Cover by Angel Achterbosch at achterbosch.net
Editing by Picky, Picky Ink
Fonts used: Johnyokonysm, Garamond

ISBN: 978-1-945135-01-9
Library of Congress Control Number: 2016914496
Printed in the United States of America

This is a work of fiction. Shelby and Cole and their family came out of my imagination, as did all the other people in this story. The *Sea Otter* is not a real boat, though it reminds me of a boat I once knew. Soapy Smith really lived and ran Skagway with his mob of vigilantes. The Chilkoot Trail was the path gold miners took into the Klondike in the great gold rush of 1898.

For David,

Let's hike it again!

Jetmore, Kansas

Jeff balanced the last bar of soap atop his pyramid display. He straightened his string tie, and turned to face the midway. The smell of popcorn and candied apples filled the air. It might be 1884, but a fair like this took him back to his boyhood in the 1870s.

"Ladies and gentlemen! Boys and girls!" Jeff called with the loud voice of a midway barker. People wanted a show? He'd give them a show. "Step right up! Right this way! Make room now!"

A few people paused to see what he was selling, but no one gathered round.

Jeff didn't mind. He knew he could pull their attention from the Watkins man and the bearded lady. All he needed was charm, a helper or two, and a little sleight of hand.

"Step right up and witness the most spectacular, the most amazing improvement in soap the world has ever seen!"

Bobo wandered toward the table, but stopped to give space for actual customers to stand in front of him. "What's so great about your soap?" Bobo shouted.

"I'm glad you asked," Jeff answered. "It cleans your house. It cleans your clothes. It cleans your dishes. And it won't chap your hands!" Jeff held his hands high in the air to show how unchapped they were. Not that he ever used the soap he was peddling. It gave him hives.

Four women dragged their husbands over. A policeman stopped to watch.

It upped the challenge, but Jeff had fooled more than one officer in his time. "Behold my shirt!" Jeff stroked the collar of his brand new white shirt showing above his black woolen vest. "I've worn this shirt every day for a year, washed it only with this special soap formula, and it looks good as new!"

A few more people stopped and gawked. Big Ed joined the back of the crowd and gave the nod.

"How do we know your soap works like you say it does?" Big Ed called out with his booming voice.

Jeff thrust a $50 bill in the air.

The crowd gasped. These folks had likely never seen so much money at once.

"This is how much I believe in this product. I'm going to wrap fifty dollars up with one of these bars of soap. If you buy the one wrapped in money, it's yours!"

A smattering of clapping, a hoot and a holler and he knew he had them.

He wrapped the fifty dollars around a bar of soap and held it up for everyone to see. This was when people's brains turned off and their greed kicked in. The crowd's energy stirred him up.

"I believe in this soap so much, I'll wrap up some other bills." He showed them a stack of money, a mix of twenties, tens, fives, and ones. He wrapped each bill around a bar of soap and wrapped each bar with plain brown paper.

The crowd stayed with him, watching him with eagle eyes. The policeman moved in closer.

A rim of sweat rose on Jeff's neck. This was the tricky part. He hoped he could pull off the switch with a cop watching him so closely. Nobody seemed to notice when he slipped each bill into his vest pocket. When he was done, Jeff mixed the soap in his suitcase stand. "Now who wants to buy some soap? We'll start at a dollar a bar. Prices go up as your odds improve."

A man in the front held out a dollar. He picked a bar of soap and handed it to his wife. She opened it and showed the crowd she hadn't won anything.

"Ohhhh," came the disappointed response. But not completely disappointed because their chances were better now.

Big Ed held up a dollar. "I'll take one."

The policeman took out his billy club and smacked his palm with it a couple of times.

Jeff eyed the cop. Had he seen the switch or not? Should Jeff let Big Ed win? To make a profit, they needed to stick with the routine. He'd take a gamble that the officer hadn't noticed the trick. He picked out a bar of soap and tossed it.

Big Ed caught it and ripped it open. "Ha-ha!" He held a $20 bill out for everyone to see. He danced in a little circle.

Jeff had seen this dance many, many times, but it always made him laugh. It also spurred the crowd on to buy more soap.

The policeman holstered his club and walked on.

Jeff took out his pocket handkerchief and wiped his brow. The hard part was over now. "That's right, ladies and gentlemen! There's more where that came from!"

Jeff kept his hands busy, taking people's money and handing out the soap. Bobo "won" twenty dollars, like he did at every podunk town they stopped in, and the price of soap went higher. No one else won anything. They never did.

The policeman came wandering back again. He started asking questions of the folks in the back row.

Jeff eyed him. He knew when a good thing got to looking too good. "That's it for today, folks," Jeff said. "Thanks for stopping by." He closed his suitcase and folded up its tripod stand in a blink. He was leaving town with a pocket full of cash. Two pockets, really, counting the money he'd started out with. But he had to leave quickly, before the crowd realized they'd been swindled.

The train had already pulled past the station when he caught the handle and swung himself onto the moving platform.

A long shrill whistle pierced his ears. He looked back to see the policeman from the fair chasing after the train, waving his club in the air.

"Stop the train!" the officer yelled.

But the railroad stops for no one, not even the law.

The policeman saw Jeff in the doorway of the train. He ran faster to catch up. "Get off that train, right now, you soapy scoundrel!"

Soapy. Jeff like the sound of it. He tipped his hat to the policeman, who was losing ground now against the train. He'd telegraph ahead to arrest Jeff and his gang. Well, Jeff was smarter than that. He'd get off this train long before that and head north where no one knew him.

Soapy Smith. That'd fit him nicely.

Chapter 1

Skagway, Alaska

Mom closed the book and set it on the galley table. "And that's just the beginning of the story of Soapy Smith, the sneakiest, dirtiest crook in Alaska."

Twelve-year old Shelby wasn't ready for the story to end. "You're skipping the good parts. What does he have to do with Alaska? How did he end up here?" She waved her arm to take in the scene surrounding the *Sea Otter,* the wooden ranger boat that was their home for the summer. The flat, blue waters of Chilkoot Inlet and surrounding tree-covered mountains seemed an unlikely place for a swindler like Soapy Smith to find fame.

"So many questions." Mom laughed. "Soapy Smith was a con man, but he was also a violent gangster and crime boss. You've got to remember, this was Skagway during the Gold Rush of 1898, over a hundred years ago. He ran gambling rings and telegraph scams. He controlled the government with his band of vigilantes. It was the wild west all over again."

"Epic," ten-year-old Cole said. "Did Skagway have gunslingers and duels and bank robberies?"

"All that," Dad said, "and more. In fact, Soapy Smith died in a shootout. And he wasn't the only one."

"I guess we'll have to be careful here, huh?" Shelby doubted Skagway would be as exciting as Juneau was. They'd had their fill of adventure there when she and Cole got caught up in a treasure hunt that almost got them killed. "Is it dangerous?"

Dad laughed. "You're not likely to find any gunslingers around here now. More likely hikers and fishermen and cruise ship visitors."

"Well, that's good." A twinge of disappointment surprised her. She thought she was done with adventure for a while. Not forever, but she'd been planning to take a little break after the week she'd just had.

Dad took off his crumpled pirate's hat he always wore when he was captaining the boat. He tossed it to Cole. "Run up the jolly roger, will you, matey? We're almost to Smuggler's Cove."

Smuggler's Cove? The name stirred her imagination.

Maybe, Shelby thought, just maybe she was ready for another adventure already.

As soon as they tied off to the dock, Mom sent Shelby and Cole for fruit and milk, but Shelby had other plans in mind. They wouldn't need the food until dinnertime, so why rush? She looked down Broadway and breathed in the old west and the call of the wild.

With Mom busy on her research project and Dad doing small repairs on the *Sea Otter*, Shelby and Cole were free to find a rip-roaring, gun-slinging, gold rush adventure of their own. The main street of Skagway, with its boardwalks and swinging saloon doors, held the promise of excitement. The days of Soapy Smith and his gang didn't seem so far behind.

Up ahead, she spotted a train that could have been out of one of the old west movies Dad liked, the kind of movie where you'd expect to see a train robbery and a good guy in a white hat galloping up on his horse to save the day.

Cole spotted the train, too, and bolted for it. He climbed aboard.

Shelby looked it over. It wasn't an old steam engine at all. It was shiny and black, with a huge red tube on the front, almost as tall as the engine car. Inside the red pipe was a giant fan or propeller or drill or something. What was this thing? She backed up to get a big-picture look. Behind the engine was a black box car with the words "White Pass" on it and, behind that, a faded red

9

caboose. The three cars sat on tracks that didn't go anywhere, right next to tracks that did.

The doors to the engine had stairs that pulled down, but they were locked in the up position to keep kids from climbing them. That, of course, didn't stop Cole.

"There's no way in up here!" he shouted. He jumped down and ran around to climb aboard the caboose.

Shelby took another step back. A train that wasn't a train with a front end that looked like a weapon from a superhero cartoon. Could this be the key to their next adventure?

"It's a snowplow."

Shelby turned at the sound of voice.

A ranger stood behind her, a thin young woman with a hat like Smokey Bear. "They use it to clear snow off the tracks in winter. See the chute?"

Sure enough, on top of the big red pipe was a red chute for blowing snow away from the tracks.

"So, it's just a snowplow?" Shelby couldn't hide the disappointment in her voice.

"Yep. They park it here for the summer. Climb on the caboose it you want. I can take your picture with your brother."

"Sure, okay." Shelby handed the ranger her phone and climbed aboard.

Just a snowplow. Lame.

She put on a straight face for the picture, like they used to do in those brown and white pictures from the old west. She jumped down, took her phone from the ranger, and turned around. "Come on, pardner," she said to Cole. "Let's go." There was no adventure to be had on a train that didn't even move.

Cole pointed to a woman dressed in a frilly red skirt and a tight black top. "Let's see where she's going."

The lady had a fancy comb in her hair and a feather boa wrapped around her shoulders. Her button-up boots clapped against the wooden sidewalk.

Shelby had never seen anyone dressed so silly, but a fancy lady like that was sure to be heading somewhere interesting. "Okay. Let's go!"

Cole hurried to catch up. Only a few doors down, the woman turned in at the Red Onion Saloon. Shelby peered in the window. The inside of the bar was all done up like the olden days. "I bet she's a dance-hall girl. Maybe she does the cancan."

Shelby was about to push through the front door of the Red Onion to go inside when the lady in red whooshed back out. She clomped around the corner of the building.

Shelby and Cole followed her, far enough back so she wouldn't notice.

The lady leaned against the wall, her back to them.

A man stood facing her. His tattered cowboy hat shielded his eyes. He hooked his thumbs in the pockets of his black velvet vest.

11

Shelby scooted forward to hear what he had to say.

The lady propped one foot up on a bench next to her and tore at her boot laces. "Stupid shoes. I don't think I'll ever break them in."

The man crossed his arms. "How come you're off so quick?"

"I just came to pick up my phone. I forgot it earlier."

"So, how come you're dressed for work?"

"I'm doing a shift over at Liarsville tonight. Give me a lift?"

"Sure. I'm supposed to be meeting someone, but I can catch him later on Skype."

Shelby deflated. The costumes might look like the old west, but the words coming out of their mouths were as modern as this morning's breakfast. They were just actors or something, dressed up as part of their job.

"Let's go, Cole." Shelby turned away from the dance-hall girl.

Up Broadway, they found some great shops, but no adventure. The news depot where she thought she'd find a printing press at work turned out to be a bookstore. She bought a book about Soapy Smith. If Mom wouldn't tell her the end of the story, she'd read it for herself.

They found a shop that sold photos, and lots with t-shirts and jewelry. Great stuff, but not exactly adventurous.

Almost at the edge of town, they gave up on adventure in favor of fudge. Shelby plunked down on a bench and unwrapped her piece of Gold Rush fudge, full of chocolate chips and peanut butter. She handed half to Cole, who immediately crammed the whole piece into his mouth. She took a small bite of hers and rolled it around in her mouth while she thought. "There's got to be more to Skagway than this," she said. "Mom said it was a rugged town, run by gangs and vigilantes."

"*Was.*" Cole wiped his mouth with his wrist.

Maybe he was right. Maybe the wild, wild west had been tamed.

Disappointed, Shelby took another nibble of fudge. In Juneau, adventure had found her the very first day when she found the chunk of ice with the compass trapped inside. Maybe Skagway's adventure wouldn't be as easy to spot. Or maybe there was no adventure to be found here at all.

Cole left the bench and trotted across the street.

Shelby looked to see what had caught his eye.

On the corner, a young woman in old-time miner clothes was setting up a tripod with a table on top. She unfurled a signed that read "The Illusive Emma Goldsbury!"

"Come one! Come all!" she cried. "Witness the magic of the Illusive Emma Goldsbury! Experience the adventures of the Great White North! Discover gold with me!"

Bingo!

Shelby crumpled her fudge wrapper, stuffed it in her pocket, and crossed the street.

Magic, adventure, and gold all in one place? Shelby was all in.

Chapter 2

The Illusive Emma Goldsbury smoothed a red velvet cloth over her improvised table.

Shelby sidled up next to Cole, close enough to see the wrinkles of the cloth flatten out under the street magician's palm. A little magic was just what she needed to brighten up a disappointing day.

Emma placed three black cups upside down on the table. She hooked her thumbs through her suspenders, rocked back on her heels and shouted, "Come one! Come all! Get a front row seat for the latest gold rush!"

Shelby looked around. There weren't any seats out here on the sidewalk, of course, but Emma was already drawing a little crowd even though she hadn't even done anything yet. The street magician wasn't anything special to look at—25 years old or so, mousy brown hair and a slightly crooked nose. But Shelby couldn't take her eyes off her. She didn't wear a cape and top hat like you'd expect, but brown corduroys, a flannel shirt, suspenders, and a crumpled red hat.

Emma pushed her sleeves up to her elbows and held out her palms to the crowd. With a twist of her wrist, a coin appeared between her fingers.

Cole whooped and clapped his hands.

Emma smiled at him. "Would you like to assist me?"

Cole grinned and nodded.

Shelby wished Emma had picked her instead.

"Watch carefully," Emma said. She placed the coin on the little table and covered it with one of the three black cups. "Don't lose it." She moved the middle cup to the left, then to the right, then switched the two end cups. Her hands flicked about, mixing the cups up with each other.

Shelby was careful to keep her eye on the cup that held the coin. No matter how fast Emma moved, if Shelby watched the one cup that mattered, she didn't have to follow the other two.

After several seconds, Emma stopped moving the cups. She held one hand over them, letting it hover while she looked at the audience. "Do you know where the coin is?"

Shelby knew. It was on the right. She was sure of it.

Cole pointed to the one Shelby was thinking of. "It's right there."

Emma moved her hand to hover over the cup Cole picked. "This one?"

"Yeah."

Emma moved her hands to the other two cups and picked them both up at the same time. Nothing under them. So he was right. She went back to the cup that was left, the one the coin would be under, and picked it up with a flourish.

A coin rested on the cloth, but instead of a quarter, it was a golden dollar. Emma picked it up between her thumb and forefinger and held it up for the crowd to see. "It's the dream of the Klondike," she said. "You come with nothing but hope and you leave with pockets full of gold." She tossed the coin to Cole.

He caught it between both hands. "Whoa!"

Shelby blinked. She'd been watching carefully the whole time, but she had somehow lost track of the quarter. When did Emma make the switch? Was it actually magic? Shelby motioned for Cole to show her the golden coin, but he stuffed it in his pocket.

Emma pulled another coin out of thin air and tossed it on the table. "Who thinks they can follow this one?"

Shelby stuck her hand in the air. She had followed the last one easily. She'd sure like a shot at a golden dollar.

Emma pointed to an older man. "You, sir. Would you like to try?"

He stepped forward and made a show of cleaning his glasses.

Crum. He couldn't even see. Of course he wouldn't be able to follow the trick.

The Illusive Emma went through the same routine as before, mixing up the cups as she moved them around on the table.

The old man chose where he thought the coin was hidden. Shelby knew he was right, and when Emma picked up the cup, she revealed the quarter she'd placed under it moments before. No golden dollar for this guy.

"Now you see how easy the game is," Emma said. "Watch carefully and place your bet. Think you know where the coin is?"

"Five bucks!" offered a man in the back.

"I'm sorry, sir. That's not worth my time. You've already seen me get beat by a kid and an old man. No offense, sir," she said, nodding to the man she'd just played. "Surely you don't think they're better than you?"

The man dug in his pocket. "Ten, then."

Shelby looked at Emma long enough to see a glimmer in her face. Ten dollars didn't sound like that much, even to Shelby, but the street magician's mood had shifted. It didn't take long to see why.

Emma handily won the bet and pocketed the cash. She roped in another bet, and then another. The next four got their money taken. On the fifth try, Emma lost the bet and made a big show of handing a $20 bill over to the happy winner. She won the next seven bets in a row and, before Shelby could add up all the winnings in her head, the young magician folded up her table, tucked it under her arm, and strolled away down the sidewalk.

The crowd scattered, leaving Shelby and Cole alone.

"That was cool!" Cole said. He held up his golden dollar.

Shelby snatched it from him. "Let me see that." She bit it. It was real.

"Hey! That's mine!" Cole grabbed it back.

Shelby let him. Something wasn't right. The Illusive Emma had made over $600 in less than 15 minutes, and Shelby was pretty sure magic didn't have anything to do with it.

Chapter 3

Shelby picked three plastic cups from the galley cupboard and set them upside down on the *Sea Otter's* table. She fished a coin out of her pocket and slapped it on the table.

"Whatcha doing?" Cole slid onto the bench opposite her.

"I'm going to figure out how that magician snookered all those people out of their money if it takes me all night." Shelby picked up the coin and tried to move it over her knuckles like she'd seen magicians do, but it was harder than it looked. The quarter got stuck on her second knuckle. When she wiggled to get it moving again, it fell, bounced off the table with a *clink!* and rolled under the table.

Cole scrambled to pick it up. "What do you mean snookered? It was magic!"

"I don't think so. Her only trick was tricking all those people out of their money."

"But I got a dollar. And that other guy—"

"Was a setup." Shelby covered the coin with the middle cup and slid the cup along the table. "Just like how Soapy Smith used to let a couple of people find money in the soap to make people think he was honest. I think Emma Goldsbury let one person win the game to make everyone else think they'd have a chance of winning. The beauty of it is, she'll have a completely different crowd every day she does her little show. She can fool the visitors off the cruise ships since they're only here for a day. They only get to see her perform once, but we're here for a week. We can watch her every day. I'll bet we can catch her slipping up. Which cup?"

Cole pointed to the right cup and he hadn't even been paying attention.

"How'd you know?"

"I can hear the coin sliding on the table."

"That's probably why she uses a cloth." Shelby found a dish towel and spread it on the table. "Watch closely this time. I'm going to try to fool you." She slid the cups around as fast as she could, but they got stuck on the towel. She pulled one close to the table's edge and tried to let the coin drop out from under the cup into her lap.

"Hey! No cheating!" Cole scooped the cups toward him. "Let me try. I'll show you how it's done."

"How what's done?" Dad leaned against the door between the galley and the pilothouse. "What's your project?"

Cole piped up first. "We saw a magician and she made lots of money. We're gonna learn how she does it so we can get rich!"

Shelby cut in. "I think she was cheating, but I don't know how. If I can figure out how the trick is done, I think I can catch her at it next time."

"The old shell game, huh? That's appropriate. Shelby. Shell game. Get it?"

"Got it." *Ugh.* "Why the *old* shell game?" Shelby tried making the coin disappear up her sleeve.

It hit the floor and rolled under Dad's foot. He picked it up. "It's a popular trick. The performer sets it up like a magic trick or a gambling game, but it's really a scam." With the flick of his wrist, he made the coin disappear.

"Wait, what— How'd you do that?" He made it look so easy, but Shelby couldn't see how it was done. "Where'd it go?"

"Where'd what go?" Now it was Mom in the galley doorway. "What else is disappearing?"

"This," Dad said, as he reached behind Cole's ear and produced the missing coin.

"What do you mean, what else?" Shelby asked.

Cole grabbed the coin from Dad. "Whoa! Can I keep it?"

Mom nodded to Cole, then turned to Shelby. "Things are going missing, odd things."

"Hey, that's my quarter!" Shelby grabbed at Cole, but he scurried to the other end of the room. She'd chase him down and wrestle it out of him, but she suddenly had bigger things on her mind. "What kind of odd things, Mom?"

"An old scale from the museum. They used to use it to weigh the gold from the Klondike Gold Rush."

"Why steal an old scale? Why not get a new one?" Cole asked. He tossed the quarter in the air and caught it, eying Shelby to see if she would chase him for it.

She wasn't biting. "Maybe it's valuable."

"Or," Dad put in, "maybe they want to get some gold of their own."

"What gold?" Shelby asked. "The Gold Rush was more than a hundred years ago."

"There's still gold in them thar hills," Dad said. He was trying to sound like a miner, maybe, but it sounded just like his pirate voice.

"There's really gold left?" Cole said.

Shelby added, "I thought it was all gone. Why aren't people looking for it?"

Mom said, "It's not laying around in the streams for people to pick up any more. If you want gold now, you're going to have to have a lot of money and fancy equipment and more than a little grit."

Shelby said, "I bet Dad's right, then. I bet they're looking for gold." She wouldn't mind finding some gold herself.

"It's a thought," Mom said, "but there are other things missing too."

"Like what?"

"Like a couple of blowtorches and a bunch of lead fishing weights from the hardware store. I mean, lead is cheap. And heavy. Why would anyone steal lead?"

Shelby thought about the list. A scale, some fishing weights. It didn't make sense. "What did they leave behind? What *should* have been stolen?"

"Well, at the museum, they left the gold pan and letters that were with the scale, all more valuable than the scale. And at the hardware store . . ." Mom turned on her phone and fiddled with it for a few seconds. She turned the phone around. "They left this."

The picture on the phone showed the floor near a shelf. The floor was empty except for one golden dollar.

Shelby stared at the coin in the photo. A golden dollar. Could it be this easy?

"Hey!" Cole said. "That's like mine."

"I know who did it!" Shelby said. "It was Emma!"

"Emma?" Dad sat down next to Mom and took the phone for a closer look at the picture.

"Emma Goldsbury. She gave Cole a dollar just like this one for playing the shell game. It's gotta be her. Show them"

Cole dug the dollar out of his pocket and held it out.

Shelby couldn't believe she could figure it out so quickly. She reached for her own phone. "So, should I call the police or are you?"

Dad laughed. "Gold-en. Not gold. These coins are made out of some kind of alloy."

That was not the reaction Shelby expected. "Who cares what they're made out of. It's her I know it's her. She's a thief and a cheater."

Mom shook her head. "You can't call the police just because you saw someone who had a dollar coin. It's legal tender. There are probably a hundred people in town with dollar coins in their pockets or in a jar at home. It's like leaving a nickel or a dollar bill behind."

"But it's not a nickel or a dollar bill. It's a gold coin. Not real gold, but fake gold. She's a trickster. It's her. I know it."

Dad laughed again. "Well, maybe it is and maybe it isn't, but we don't have enough reason to call the police on her." He fished in his pocket and pulled out a golden dollar. "Do you think I'm a thief?"

"No." Of course she didn't. He had a point. The gold coin wasn't proof enough. She'd just have to find more. Fine with her. She wanted to go watch the Illusive Emma do her tricks again anyway.

"And, Shelby?" Dad looked her straight in the eye. "Don't go trying to catch anyone on your own. Leave it to the adults this time, okay?"

"We solved the last mystery." Was it only last week that she and Cole had found the necklace that had been hidden for a hundred years?

"With some help and a lot of good luck," Mom said. "You could have died. Leave the crime fighting to the professionals. Promise?"

Shelby heaved a sigh. If she didn't promise, she'd be stuck hanging out on the boat all day. But if she did, she'd have to keep her promise. After what happened in Juneau, she didn't plan to lie to her parents again.

Ever.

There must be a way to tell the truth and still catch Emma in the act. Mom just said not to fight crime. She didn't say not to do a little sleuthing around.

"Okay, Mom. I promise. I won't try to catch anyone." It wasn't a lie.

She just wanted to prove Emma was cheating at the shell game. She didn't even have to prove she was the thief, even though she was, for sure. Anyway, she could figure out how the magician did the coin trick from the safety of the crowd.

There was no danger in that.

Chapter 4

S helby and Cole looked for the Illusive Emma Goldsbury the next morning on the same corner as the day before. She wasn't there. They looked all up and down Broadway, checking every doorway, peering into every window.

A newspaper dispenser held the town paper. Shelby checked the headlines for news of the theft, but it wasn't mentioned. She checked the date. The paper was nearly a week old.

"Maybe it wasn't Emma," Cole said, carefully hopping over every crack in the sidewalk.

"Oh, it was her, all right." Shelby was sure of it.

They didn't find the magician on the corner across from the fudge factory, either.

"Let's check that out!" Cole pointed to a sign advertising a place to pan for gold. "You think it's real?"

"I don't know," Shelby said. "Let's find out."

They raced the two blocks to where a prospector had set up a trough filled with water.

"Is there really gold in there?" Cole asked.

You couldn't really see down through the water.

"Darn tootin'," the miner said. He wore the same kind of flannel shirt and wool pants as Emma Goldsbury, and he had a long, white grizzled beard. He scooped his pan into the water and pulled up a glob of black sand. "Guaranteed gold in every pan."

Shelby asked Cole, "Want to split our findings?"

"Sure." He looked in his pockets for money, but came up empty except for the golden dollar. "Can' I pay you back later?"

Shelby shelled out five dollars for the chance to go home with a gold nugget. The prospector showed her how to hold the pan and swirl the water to let the heavy gold sink to the bottom and the lighter sand swish over the edge.

"You're moving it too much," he said. "Nice easy circles or you'll toss the gold right out of the pan. Let's get you a fresh batch." He used the gold pan to scoop up another load of sand. "Easy now. Take your time."

Shelby concentrated on making small circles.

Cole said, "You're taking too long. Come on, my turn!"

Shelby ignored him. She couldn't wait to see that gold nugget appear in the bottom of the pan. Instead, for all her effort, she got a teaspoon full of iron shavings. "No gold," she said.

She thought Cole would jump in for his turn, but he'd wandered off to climb on the playground across the street.

The prospector leaned in. "Sure you got gold. Look, see?" He pointed a dirty finger at a fleck of yellow so small you could hardly see it.

"Where?" Cole leaned in really close.

"That's gold?" Shelby squinted at it.

"Straight out of the hills."

She touched the fleck with her fingertip. The little speck stuck and she brought it to her eye. "I thought it would be bigger. Let's bigger."

He laughed. "So did everyone who risked life and limb. A handful found nuggets, but most found flakes like that one. You can take it with you." He opened a tiny glass vial and filled it with water.

Shelby stuck her finger to the lip of the vial. Her miniature grain of gold sank to the bottom.

The miner capped the vial and handed it to her. "Find a million more like that and you'll be rich."

Shelby reached in her pocket for a piece of string. She threaded it through the vial's cap and tied it around her neck. It might not be much, but it was the most gold she'd ever owned before. She'd keep it close. "Look, Cole. I got gold."

Cole came over and squinted at it. "There's gold in there? How're we gonna split that?"

"I don't know." She didn't think there was any way to share it. She reckoned it was really hers since she'd paid the money and done the work. "It's real gold, though."

"Next gold we find is mine," he said.

If it was all this tiny, fine with her.

"I wanna find some real gold, like a big chunk of it."

"Still has the power to turn a sane man's head." The voice came from above. Shelby turned and raised her eyes up and up to see who was talking. The first thing she saw was his horse, then his bright red uniform. His black pants had a sharp yellow stripe down the side.

"Who are you s'posed to be?" asked Cole, tipping his head all the way back to see way up in the air.

"That there's a Canadian Mountie," said the prospector.

"Royal Canadian Mounted Police," said the man on the horse. "Roberts."

"How are you s'posed to sneak up on bad guys when you're so bright red?" Cole asked. "I bet they can see you a mile away."

"Helps us not get confused for moose in the woods, I guess," the Mountie said. "Good luck on your hunt for gold. Keep your nose clean," he tipped his hat, "and have a good day." He spun his horse away from the kids and clopped off up the street.

Cole brushed at his nose.

A fresh batch of would-be miners crowded up to the trough, squeezing Shelby and her brother out.

"Guaranteed gold in every pan!" the prospector announced.

"Come on, Cole," Shelby said. "Let's go find that magician."

"And some gold," Cole added.

And gold, of course. But Shelby still wanted to figure out the trick.

They found the Illusive Emma Goldsbury mid-morning on a corner close to the docks.

"Stay in the back and stay quiet," Shelby warned Cole. He fidgeted every time Emma called for volunteers.

"Hush!" she whispered. "We don't want her to notice us." Shelby wanted to watch Emma's trick as many times as she could. If they drew attention to themselves, she'd never even get the chance to see the trick again much less figure out how it was done.

The routine went down exactly like the day before. One person won a dollar. Then four or five people lost. Then someone won $20 and then everyone else lost. It was definitely a pattern. Shelby tried to remember who the winner was yesterday. If it was the same person, then Shelby could prove it was a scam. She couldn't quite recall the lady's face from the day before. This one looked older, she thought, but she'd have to watch the show one more time to be sure. She snapped a picture of the lady who won the $20 so she could compare her face with the winner at the next show. She tucked her phone back in her pocket and pretended to be amazed whenever another person lost.

Shelby watched for a slip-up in the shell game. She knew the magician was switching out coins under those black cups, but Emma's hands were too quick. The Illusive Emma Goldsbury lived up to her name— Illusive *and* elusive. From the back row in the crowd, Shelby watched her hands as closely as she could, but she never could tell where the sleight of hand took place. It didn't help that a tall man in a clear plastic rain poncho kept leaning into her line of sight.

Emma packed up her little suitcase with Shelby none the wiser.

Cole wanted to look for gold in the river near town after lunch, but once Shelby set her mind to solving a mystery, she was like a bloodhound on the trail. Emma was pulling the same scam as Soapy Smith, and Shelby was going to figure out how. He'd started out cheating people on street corners and ended up running a town like a mobster. Maybe Emma was heading the same way. Shelby dragged Cole back along the street with the promise of either adventure or ice cream, whichever came first.

It didn't take long to find Emma on the same corner as yesterday, across from the fudge factory. She unfolded her stand and set her suitcase on top of it, unfurled the banner with her name across it, and spread out the red velvet cloth. She called out, just like yesterday and this morning.

"Come one! Come all! Witness the magic of the Illusive Emma Goldsbury and experience the adventures of the Great White North!"

Shelby stayed across the street until a few people had gathered. She wanted a better view than this morning, but not front and center. She had a few more minutes before the show would start. By now she knew exactly what to expect.

But after Emma called out a few more times, she reached down and picked up something Shelby wasn't expecting, a blue canister with a nozzle.

Shelby's eyebrow shot up. Was that—? Could it be—? "Come on, Cole. We gotta get closer," she said. She raced across the street to get a better look.

It was a small blue blowtorch. Aha!

Shelby watched closely. "Take a picture!" she whispered to Cole.

"Of what?" he whispered back.

"Of the blowtorch. Isn't that one of the things that got stolen?"

While Cole got out his phone to take a picture, Shelby watched Emma's hands as carefully as she could.

From out of nowhere, Emma produced a small sphere of clay.

Shelby gasped. It couldn't possibly be a coincidence.

"I have in my hands an ordinary lump of clay," Emma said. "Would anyone care to inspect it?"

Shelby gave Cole the eye to keep him from raising his hand. Let an adult do the inspecting. Let the kids stay invisible.

A short man stepped forward and took the clay. He squashed it between his thumb and forefinger and gave a nod to the crowd. "Looks okay to me," he said and handed it back to Emma.

The magician rolled her hands together and formed the piece of clay back into a perfect ball. "Watch closely," she said, picking up some kind of mold from the corner of her table. She slammed the clay into the mold and pressed it with the heel of her hand. Then she clapped another mold on the other side and pressed the two together. She set the mold on the red velvet. "Here's where I should wave my magic wand," she said, passing one hand back and forth through the air over the mold. "If I had a magic wand. Instead I will use my magic fingers. A volunteer, please?"

The same little man stepped forward and, following her directions, helped release the clay from its mold. It looked just like a coin, only it was made out of gray clay.

"Now for the magic," the Illusive Emma said.

Shelby leaned in closer. She didn't want to miss a thing.

Emma fired up the little blowtorch. And inch-long flame shot out of the nozzle. Emma held it up for everyone to see. "You've heard of alchemy, the ability

34

to turn ordinary materials into gold? Until now, it's only been a dream, but I have learned the secret!"

The crowd pressed in for a closer look.

Emma passed the flame over the clay coin, back and forth, back and forth. As she did, she kept up a lively banter, asking questions of the crowd and fielding their shouted answers.

Shelby tried not to blink. The trick had to happen when the crowd was distracted. Well, Shelby would not be fooled.

To her disappointment and surprise, and then to her delight, the coin in front of her slowly changed colors. The gray seemed to melt away. Sparling, yellow gold took its place. She was making pure gold right before their eyes. Maybe the Illusive Emma was for real. Maybe she could produce gold out of thin air. But if she could, why would she steal the supplies to do it? Why not pay for them with the gold she was making?

Emma turned off the torch. She picked up the coin with a pair of tongs and dipped it in a bowl of water. The water sizzled and sent up a puff of steam. "She's real, folks!" Emma said. "You're welcome to touch, but not to take. You've seen the potential, now get in on the profits. Today only, you can get in on the ground floor of the biggest money making venture north of Antarctica. Partner with me and together we can become very, very rich."

The man who had volunteered stepped to the table first. He bit the coin. "It's the real thing. I'm in!" He set the coin back on the table and pulled out his checkbook. "How much?"

Everyone who touched the coin had the same reaction. People were writing checks left and right, handing over $100 bills, and signing papers that Emma had on hand for anyone who wanted to invest. It must be real gold. You couldn't fool so many people at once. Not up close like that. Shelby eased forward for her chance to hold the coin. When she picked it up she was surprised by its weight, but even more by how soft it felt, nothing like the tinny coins that rattled around in her pocket or the chunky golden dollar Cole had taken home yesterday. This metal seemed alive. No wonder people went so crazy over it.

She flipped it over. It was obviously handmade, not a coin like you'd find at a coin shop, but one that was unique, like the old, old Roman ones she'd seen in Grumpa's collection of odd treasures. Emma just might be the real deal.

Shelby reluctantly set the coin back on the table.

A thin, tall woman picked it up. She looked like a gypsy with loose velvety clothing and dozens of necklaces and bracelets, a real artsy type. She even had the kind of gnarled hands you'd expect, though her face wasn't wrinkled. The gypsy lady put the coin to her mouth and bit it.

The woman lowered her voice. "Metal. Clay. Magic," she whispered.

No secrets there. Emma had used magic to turn the clay to metal.

All of a sudden, Emma started cramming stuff into her suitcase. She threw in the gold coin, crumpled up the velvet cloth and stuffed it in, too. She wasn't being smooth and sneaky anymore. She fumbled with the tripod. "Show's over, folks! If you didn't invest, you missed your chance! You'll be hearing from me!" She tucked the suitcase under her arm and speed-walked up the street toward to the edge of town.

Shelby looked after her. What was it about what the gypsy lady said that made Emma run away like that? She looked at Cole, but he just shrugged.

Weird.

No one else seemed to notice the strange way the street magician took off. One man carefully folded the paper, his investment agreement she guessed, and tucked it inside of his jacket. He looked down the street at Emma's retreating back before stepping off the sidewalk in the opposite direction.

All the adults scattered, leaving Shelby and Cole alone.

"Now what?" Cole said, looking longingly back at the fudge factory.

"I'm not sure."

"Can we get some fudge and then go look for her again?"

Shelby shook her head. "She won't be back. I think the Illusive Emma Goldsbury has retired from her magical career."

"What makes you say that?"

Shelby pointed down at the sidewalk to a business card. On it was a picture of a puff of smoke and one word.

Poof!

Chapter 5

Emma Goldsbury was gone all right. But a little disappearing act didn't mean the whole thing was over. Every magic show Shelby had ever been to, the magician always came out for the final bow.

"Let's follow her," Shelby said.

"But, why?" Cole asked. "If that's her last show, there won't be anything else to see."

"It might be her last magic show, but I don't think she's done. Not by a long shot. She stole all that stuff yesterday. But if she can make her own gold, why did she need to steal?"

"I give up. Why?"

Shelby thought about it. "She's a performer. I bet she's gearing up for something bigger and better. That's why she left the golden coin at the museum, to show people who to look for, like a calling card."

"So?"

"So if we can figure out where she's gone, we can make sure there's someone to see whatever she's planning to do."

"Where are we going?" Cole tugged on Shelby's arm to turn her around. "She went the other way."

Shelby ignored him and strode doggedly back toward the harbor. "I know. That's why I'm going this way."

Cole stopped and stared at her. "Huh?"

Shelby grabbed his shirt and pulled him to get his feet moving again. "She's a magician isn't she? Whatever you think she's doing, she's probably doing the exact opposite. So if she wants us to think she's heading for the mountains, she probably went back toward the dock."

"Oh." Cole trotted ahead of her down Broadway.

Shelby looked every passing adult in the eye. She peered into every shop window she walked by, hoping to catch a glimpse of Emma. If the magician was trying to disappear, she would at least change clothes, and probably her hair, too.

Cole stared for longer than he needed to into the showgirl saloon. Shelby scooted up beside him to move him along. "She's not in there. Let's keep moving."

"She might be one of those," he said, pressing his index finger to the glass to point out a row of cancan girls.

Shelby pressed her forehead to the window for a closer look. "None of those looks even close," she said. "Come on." She pulled him away from the window and down the sidewalk toward the harbor. Cruise ship passengers still crowded the shops and roads. What if Emma's plan was to catch one of the ships and trick her captive audience out of their money? If she decided to hitch a ride on one of them, Shelby and Cole would never find her, much less be able to stop her.

If her audience was captive, though, it meant she was too. She wouldn't trap herself like that.

Shelby scrutinized the faces around her even more closely. Where could Emma have gone?

"Look!" Cole shouted. He pointed and waved his arm toward a white building down and across the street. "I think she went in there!"

"Are you sure?" Shelby looked both ways, then bolted across the street before Cole could answer.

A sign painted on top of the building said "White Pass and Yukon Route." A bench sat outside. Above the bench was a set of wooden signs that told departure times for the trains leaving Skagway. Made sense, she'd be looking for a way out of town. A train was as good a way as any. Both of these trains would take her up and over the mountains out of Skagway and out of the United States into Canada.

Cole ran up beside her, panting. "Not here. There." He pointed to the building next door.

So, not the train after all?

Shelby walked up the sidewalk to get a look at the name of this building.

Way up top, it said "Railroad Building," but the writing on the windows said, "Klondike Gold Rush National Historic Park."

Why in the world would someone trying to get out of town go to a museum? The train made a lot more sense.

"Are you sure she went in this one?" Shelby asked.

"I'm sure," Cole said. "I mean, I'm sure it was this building. I'm not sure it was her. The lady I saw wasn't dressed like a magician. She looked like she was going camping or hunting or something."

"Let's check it out." Shelby opened the door and stepped inside. It took a minute to adjust to the dim light after being in the sunshine. A few people were milling around, looking at the huge old black-and-white photos on the walls.

Shelby went up to the desk to speak to the ranger on duty. "Have you seen a lady with long hair and . . ." How was she supposed to describe Emma Goldsbury? There was nothing remarkable about her except her ability to trick people. "She's a magician and I think I saw her come in here."

The ranger, in full khaki and a ranger hat, looked up at Shelby and then looked around the crowded room. "Not Emma Goldsbury?"

Shelby couldn't believe her luck. "Yeah. That's her! You know her? Is she here?"

The ranger looked around again. "I saw her a minute ago. She must have just left."

Shelby couldn't believe they'd missed her. "Did you see which way she went?"

"The trail center, I assume. For her permit."

Shelby thought for sure they'd find her in here, but she was always a step ahead. "Where's the trail center?"

"Up Broadway. Past the Artworks. You can't miss it." He pointed in the general direction.

Shelby dashed out the door, Cole just ahead of her. She jogged back down to the main street and found the building with a sign out front that read "Trail Center."

"She's got to be in there," Shelby said.

"What if she's not?" Cole asked.

"She's gotta." Shelby didn't know where they'd look next if this spot wasn't right. She and Cole let themselves in. The room was pretty open. No Emma Goldsbury here, and nowhere for her to hide.

"Can I help you with something?" It was the lady ranger who had showed them the huge snowplow when they first got into town the day before.

"I was just looking—" Shelby started, but Cole interrupted her.

"Where's the magician?"

"Emma? She just left," said the ranger.

Ah, man. They'd missed her again. Shelby turned toward the door. If they left now, maybe they wouldn't be too late to find her.

The ranger's voice pulled her back. "You don't even want to know if I know where she's going?"

Shelby stopped in her tracks. She'd given up too easily. She turned back toward the ranger. "Do you? Where?"

The ranger tapped the ledger book on the counter in front of her. "She's heading up the Chilkoot Trail. Just left here with her permit."

"What's the Chilkoot Trail?" Shelby asked at the same time Cole said, "Where's that?"

The ranger grinned and held up her hand. "Whoa! One question at a time. First of all, my name is Robyn. What's yours?"

"Cole," Cole said. "And that's my sister Shelby."

"Great meeting you. Now, the Chilkoot Trail is the one gold seekers took to get them up into Canada during the Klondike Gold Rush of 1898. Thirty-three miles on foot took them to Lake Bennett where they could build a boat and float up into the Yukon and look for gold. It's a tough hike."

"And people still take that trail?" Shelby felt the pull of hills full of gold.

"Yup. Emma's starting tomorrow. I'll be hiking in tomorrow, too. It's my turn on duty at Sheep Camp. That's a long day's walk in. Most people stop at Canyon City the first night. It's a tough hike."

"Not too tough for me," Cole boasted.

Ranger Robyn laughed. "I'm sure you're right. You look pretty strong."

"I am," he said. "At least he didn't put his arms out to show his muscles. "We should climb it," he said to Shelby.

She'd had exactly the same thought. If Emma was going to be on the trail, they should be as well. "How much for a permit?" she asked.

Ranger Robyn shook her head. "Sorry, kids. We only allow 50 people a day on the trail, plus some day-users. Tomorrow's permits have been sold out for months. Emma probably paid for hers back in the winter."

Shelby just couldn't seem to make any headway in catching up with the Illusive Emma. Talk about a trail going cold. How were they supposed to follow Emma now? "What happens if you go on the trail with no permit?"

"You get fined, anywhere from $250 up to $5,000. Some people even go to jail. Don't go without a permit. I'm the ranger on duty, you know, and I've seen your faces. I'd hate to have to write you a citation."

It seemed like another dead end. Shelby looked at Cole and shrugged. "I guess that's it, then."

"I guess."

They thanked the ranger and went outside.

"What now?" Cole said. "If we can't find gold, can we hunt for fudge?"

Tempting, but Shelby's practical side took over. "It's late. We should probably get back to the boat and see what's going on. Looks like the Illusive Emma Goldsbury eluded us after all."

"Can we look for gold on the way?"

Shelby knew any gold that used to be in Skagway town would have been discovered a hundred years ago. But she'd spent all day on her hunt. It was fair to let Cole have a turn.

They scrambled down to the edge of the Taiya River. Its cold water flowed milky blue from the glacial silt in it. They didn't have a gold pan, so they just scooped up loose sand in a water bottle and shook it, holding it up to the light to see if any specks of gold glinted at them.

Nothing.

"Guess we need a gold pan to find gold," Shelby said.

Cole shook his head. "Not if we find a big nugget."

"That's not gonna happen."

He shrugged.

They walked back toward the docks. A funny feeling washed over Shelby when she saw the *Sea Otter* in the harbor. It was almost like going home.

Mom was in the galley, filleting a salmon.

Shelby was surprised to find her there. She should be off on her research project. "How come you're here?"

Mom slid the long, thin fillet knife between skin and red meat. "Some of our equipment is missing."

"Who stole it?" Cole asked.

Mom blew a strand of hair out of her face. "I didn't say stolen. I said missing."

"What's missing, then?" Shelby asked.

Mom wiped off her hands. "A couple of electronic machines that are kind of expensive. One is to measure how tall a tree is. The other one can tell you how thick something is and what it's made of using ultrasonic waves. That one looks like a cell phone, but it costs a couple thousand dollars. I'm hoping they find it so we can get back to work."

None of those items seemed to have anything to do with the stuff that was stolen yesterday and nothing to do with Emma. "So you have to test a tree to see if it's made of wood? Can't you tell by just looking at it?"

Mom smiled. "You can use it to see if there's anything inside the tree, or how dense the tree is. You can also use it for other materials. You can also use it see if metal is pure. I think jewelers use one like it to measure the purity of gold."

Shelby's ears perked up at that. If it could be used for testing gold, Emma Goldsbury would definitely have need for it. But it was too late to prove anything,

Emma was probably already heading for the Canadian border.

"Maybe the ghost of Soapy Smith took it," Cole suggested.

Mom laughed. "If so, he's going to have a hard time collecting the reward."

Shelby's heart quickened. "There's a reward?"

"A small one. $250."

That sounded like a big reward to Shelby. She knew of plenty of things she could use that money for. But it was too late. Emma was heading out on the trail and Shelby had no way to follow her.

She flopped down at the table. The surface, normally kept clean, was covered with pouches of camping food—beef stroganoff, lasagna, spaghetti, even blueberry cobbler. Just add water.

"What's all this for?" she asked.

"Oh, that's for a little project your dad is doing. Well, actually something he's doing with you."

"What is it? Are we going camping?"

Mom cocked her head to the side. "Camping? Hmmm . . . yes, I supposed you could say that. More like hiking."

"That's a lot of food for a hike."

Mom wiped her hands on her apron. She walked over to the table and put her finger on a piece of paper on the corner. "Act surprised when he gets here, okay? He thought you'd be gone a little longer."

"What? What's the surprise?" Cole was practically jumping up and down. "Where are we going?"

Shelby looked at the paper under Mom's finger. It read Klondike Gold Rush NHP Permit.

Permit. The date on it was tomorrow.

"Is this? Is it—?"

"You're going on a hike tomorrow. Well, all week, really."

"The Chilkoot Trail?" For real?

"You've heard of it?"

"Heard of it? I've always wanted to go on it." Always as in since she heard of it this afternoon.

"When we decided to make this research trip a family trip, we knew I'd be working most of the time. Your dad wanted to do some special things with the two of you. The first thing he did was get your permits for the Chilkoot."

"Epic!" said Cole.

Shelby thought it was epic, too.

Mom looked at each of them. "This trail is no joke. It's going to be difficult. Pay attention to your dad and do whatever he asks you to. I don't want any repeats of what happened in Juneau."

"Sure, Mom," Shelby said, but her mind was racing ahead. She had another chance to prove Emma Goldsbury was the crook. She wouldn't blow it this time.

Chapter 6

Shelby intended to start the trail out strong and try to catch up with the Illusive Emma. The magician hadn't signed her name to the trail log, but why would she? The rangers in Skagway had her name on the permit. The question was, "Was Emma ahead of or behind them?" And what did she have with her that she didn't want to take through a guarded border crossing?

Shelby took off at a near sprint. Within a few minutes, the steep climb into the forest and her heavy backpack slowed her way down. She gasped for each breath.

"Not far now," Dad called cheerfully from behind her. "The first bit is a little steep, but it'll flatten out soon."

A little steep? He wasn't kidding. He'd done this trail before, but his memory could be a little fuzzy on things like how high the climb was or how much longer until they reached camp.

Cole called from above, "I'm at the top! Hurry up! And I already found my walking stick!" Every hike they went on, he found the perfect stick.

"That didn't take you long!" Shelby yelled back.

Dad chuckled. "That one's a mountain goat. Always has been."

Shelby pushed her burning legs to go a little farther, a little faster. She could be a mountain goat, too.

The trail finally leveled out. She flopped down at the edge of the path and threw her pack off. How was she supposed to catch up with Emma if she couldn't even hike ten minutes without hyperventilating?

Dad reached the top of the hill and hiked on past. "Come on, kids," he said. "That was just the first few hundred feet. We have about eight miles to go before we reach camp for the night."

"Eight miles?"

"It's level," Dad said.

Shelby knew she could do eight miles as long as it was flat. The hike up to the glacier near Juneau was about that long and she'd done it twice. She shrugged her pack back on and stood up.

"Let's go already," she said, brushing past Dad where he stood waiting for her on the path.

"Hold up," Dad called.

She stopped and waited for him and Cole to catch up with her.

"Some ground rules before we get too far. This is wild country and you need to pay attention. There are cliffs and freezing water, rock slides and avalanches. And bears."

"Cool!" Cole said. "I want to see a bear."

"You probably will," Dad said. "But you need to take precautions. First, don't ever get out of my sight. We hike together. If you want to hike ahead of me, that's fine, but don't turn the bend until I catch up with you."

Stay in sight? How was Shelby going to catch Emma if she had to hike with Dad?

"Second, don't surprise the bears."

"How do we keep from surprising them?" Shelby wanted to know.

"Make lots of noise. Sing a song. You don't want to sneak up on a bear and startle him. Or worse, her."

"Why worse?" Cole asked.

"That's number three. There is nothing more dangerous than getting between a bear and her cubs. Don't do it. If you see one bear, look around to see if there are any others."

Shelby asked, "What do we do if we see a bear?" By now she was leading the three of them along the trail.

"Depends on what kind it is. Group together. Try to look big. Back away slowly. You can sometimes scare off a black bear, but never try to scare a grizzly."

Shelby kept her eyes open for bears as they walked. Behind her, Dad and Cole sang an echo song about meeting a bear in tennis shoes. They were plenty loud to warn any bears they were coming.

After going through evergreen forest for a way, they broke out into the sunlight. A long steel bridge took them to the other side of the raging Taiya River. Not far from there, long straight boards served as bridges over a series of marshes. Dad pointed out a beaver dam. Shelby scoured the brush to try to see one, but there was no sign of the busy creatures other than a bunch of chewed-up trees.

They crossed a suspension bridge and a hundred other bridges over creeks and brooks and waterfalls. Finally, they arrived at Finnegan's Point, the first designated campsite on the trail.

"Take a little break," Dad said. "Get a snack, but don't get too comfortable. We're not staying here."

Shelby looked around, but there wasn't much to see, just a warming shelter, a bear pole for lifting your food out of reach of curious critters, and an outhouse.

And a million mosquitoes. The vicious bugs even bit through her long-sleeved shirt. Shelby dug in her backpack for her bug repellent. She sprayed herself all over—twice—and doused her arms in anti-itch juice.

Cole kept swatting at the skeeters, like he was doing some desperate war dance.

Even Dad was eager to go after only a few minutes. "Alaska state bird," he muttered.

"Where?" Shelby looked around but she didn't see any birds.

Dad slapped his neck and pulled a mosquito away in his palm. A smear of blood showed he was too late. "Here."

Shelby waved her hands in the air to shoo the bugs away. "Can we get out of here before these *birds* carry us off and eat us for dinner?"

Dad and Cole were both happy to comply. It was a long walk, but not a difficult one, to get to Canyon City. Shelby thought about Emma all the way there. What did she have in her pack that she didn't want anyone to see? It might be filled with gold, but if it was, it would be too heavy to carry. Shelby had seen her turn clay into gold. Could she just be smuggling her supplies across the border? Or was it more sinister than that?

The first thing Shelby noticed when they walked into camp was a log cabin with a picnic table out front. The second thing she saw was Emma Goldsbury eating off a golden plate. It might just be a plate, but it sure looked like one of the pieces from an old scale like that one that was stolen.

With a little spy work and some subtle conversation, that reward would be hers.

Chapter 7

Make any gold today?" Cole flopped down at the picnic table across from Emma Goldsbury and asked her straight out.

"Don't know what you mean," Emma answered. Her eyes bored through him. Did she recognize the kids from her magic show? Well, she would now that Cole had opened his big mouth.

Shelby nudged him to keep him from saying more. She needed to dispel Emma's suspicions about them. To her, they should be just a couple of kids, not the type of people who were onto her scams. She took at close look at Emma's plate. It was the right size for a camping plate, but it was made out of old metal. It had three little tabs along the edge, perfect for attaching chains for a scale. Then again, it could just be part of an old camping kit. She couldn't tell. She'd need more evidence. She blurted out the most innocent question she could think of. "Do you like s'mores?"

Emma squinted at her until she decided Shelby was safe to talk to. Her face relaxed. "Um, I guess."

"Well, we're making them tonight after dinner. We're going to have a campfire over there." Shelby pointed to the platform where Dad was unfurling the blue two-man tent he and Cole would share. Shelby still needed to pitch her own orange one. "You can come if you want."

"Maybe," Emma said. It was more than Shelby expected as far as promises go.

Dad busied himself with building a roaring fire from downed sticks Cole eagerly collected from the forest floor. The dancing red and orange flames drew a crowd. There was a skinny young German with a scruffy start to his beard who said his name was Steffan. Next to him was a couple who looked like an ad for a backpacking magazine with their matching outfits and packs. They introduced themselves as Kinsey and Ken. A few others gathered around. Dad poked at the fire. Cole roasted marshmallows on a stick he'd found earlier in the day and sharpened to a fine point with his new pocketknife.

Shelby's dinner, a bag of dehydrated chili mac, didn't look that appetizing, but she was so hungry after the day's long hike that she couldn't wait to wolf it down. While she shoveled spoonful after spoonful into her mouth, she kept on eye on Emma Goldsbury.

The magician stayed apart from everyone else. She boiled water over a camping stove and poured it into her own foil pouch of dehydrated camping food.

Shelby watched Emma through the smoke, sure she was the one who had stolen all the stuff. But why? And if she really did take the scale, why was she flaunting it in front of everyone? Maybe she thought no one on the trail would know it was missing. Or maybe she didn't think they'd recognize it. And what about her claims that she could change clay to gold? Shelby had seen it with her own eyes. If Emma really could make gold out of clay, why wasn't she back in town doing just that?

None if it made sense. Shelby kept an eye on Emma, watching for any strange behavior, while she listened to the conversation around the fire.

"Did you see the beavers?" Steffan asked. His English was good, but he still had an accent.

"Where?" asked Cole.

"Right by their den. Two of them."

"Aw man! I wish I saw it!" Cole said. "I felt a beaver skin once. It was super soft!"

Dad nodded. "Soft enough for most of the beavers in America to get trapped and skinned a hundred years before you were born."

"I saw a porcupine," Ken added. "It shot quills at me."

"Did not," countered Cole.

Emma looked toward the group circled around the fire.

Shelby watched her closely to see if the magician was giving away any clues. She was looking in her pack. Shelby pretended to look away, turning her head toward Dad, while keeping her eyes on Emma.

"Did too." Ken rummaged in his pocket and pulled out a handful of little hollow brown and white sticks.

Cole picked one up. "Cool."

Shelby reached out to touch one too. They felt like stiff little straws.

Ken pointed to the trail they'd come up. "And we saw some bears just down the river a little ways. Not far from camp."

"What kind?" It was Emma Goldsbury, standing just outside the circle of the flame's light. Shelby hadn't seen her approach. She looked totally at ease. If she was guilty, she was doing a great job of hiding it.

"Well, they were brown, but they were pretty small. So definitely not grizzlies."

"I'm terrified of brown bears," Emma said.

Shelby didn't think the magician was afraid of anything. She looked Emma straight in eye, testing her while she asked Dad, "I thought brown bears and grizzlies were the same thing?"

Ken laughed. "Brown isn't a color; it's a kind. A brown bear *is* a grizzly. Black bears can be black or brown or even cinnamon. Just remember, black bears are more scared of you than you are of them usually."

She didn't like the way he talked to her like she was dumb. She might be young, but that mean she didn't know stuff.

"What about grizzlies?" Shelby asked.

Emma piped up. "Grizzlies aren't afraid of anything."

Cole popped a marshmallow in his mouth. "How do you tell them apart?"

"There's a Forest Service warning about that," Dad said. He winked at Shelby.

Oh boy. Here we go.

Dad kept talking. "There have been a lot of grizzly bear sightings along the trail lately. And grizzlies this time of year can be pretty hungry since the salmon aren't running yet. Everyone is supposed to carry pepper spray and tie little jingly bells to their clothes."

A lot of good that advice was now that they were already out in the wilderness. Shelby didn't have a single bell with her, just the whistle Dad insisted she strap to her pack.

"But how do you tell them apart?" Steffan asked. "Size, I know."

And their hump, Shelby thought. Grizzlies have a hump on their shoulders.

But Dad didn't say anything about the hump. Instead he said, "You have to look at their droppings."

Shelby rolled her eyes. Like she was going to look for the bear's scat when it was charging her.

"Black bear droppings are smaller. Sometimes they have berries or bits of fur in them. Or even leaves."

"Gross," said Cole.

Kinsey made a face, too. "What about grizzlies?"

"Grizzly bear droppings are bigger. They smell like pepper spray." Dad grinned even bigger. "Oh, and they are full of little bells."

Steffan's face changed from looking sick to puzzled. When he finally got it, he smacked his forehead. Even Emma laughed out loud.

When Shelby looked at her, though, Emma turned quickly away.

"That's the show for tonight, folks!" Dad said, pleased with himself that his joke had gone over so well. "Same time, same price tomorrow night at Sheep Camp. Be there or be square."

"Oh, we'll be there," Ken said. Kinsey nodded in agreement. Steffan and even Emma promised to join them the next night.

"What brought you all on this trail?" Dad asked of the group. "I hiked it when I was a kid and have always wanted to bring my kids on it. How 'bout you?"

"I came all the way from Germany just to hike the Chilkoot," Steffan replied.

Ken spoke up. "This is our forty-seventh trail. We're writing a book."

"We're doing a hundred," Kinsey added. "Trails, that is."

Shelby didn't have any reason to dislike them, but something about the way they talked told her they thought they were better than her.

Shelby turned away from them to hear why Emma was on the Chilkoot—or at least why she would say she was.

But Emma wasn't there. She had quietly left the circle and gone back to her own tent. Shelby could see her crouching near the platform her tent sat on. When she looked back toward the fire, her eyes glowed with worry. Emma was up to something, for sure, and it looked like whatever it was had been hidden under her tent.

Shelby found a coin in her pocket and rubbed it between her thumb and fingers. Whatever Emma was up to, Shelby wouldn't rest until she figured it out.

Chapter 8

Shelby drew her sleeping bag up to her chin. She squeezed her eyes shut, but the late night sun glowed orange through the sides of her tent and through her eyelids. She couldn't stop thinking about what Emma must have hidden under her platform. If the sun would ever set, she meant to find out.

She could almost taste that reward money.

A twig snapped nearby, a reminder that even if the people all fell asleep, the woods were full of other critters. She wondered if the food smells would draw bears here in the night. They'd stashed their food in metal lockers designed to keep the bears out, but couldn't the bears smell the dinner they had eaten? Had Cole burned his marshmallow stick or would the bears come looking for s'mores?

Every sound in the forest made her jump. In the distance, a loon cried its mournful call. A rodent scuffled under the wooden platform Shelby lay on. It couldn't get into the tent unless it gnawed its way in.

She imagined it chewing on the fabric and letting itself in to share the small space with her.

Was that the sound of Dad snoring or was a grizzly snuffling around looking for a tasty late-night snack of a young girl wrapped in a sleeping bag like a pig in a blanket?

Just Dad, she told herself.

The sun was taking its time setting. Her eyelids felt heavy. She fought to stay awake, but it was a fight she couldn't win. The light faded enough that everything inside the tent took on a shade of dark gray. She would just rest her eyes for a minute, then she would steal a look at whatever Emma was hiding. She'd only close her eyes, not let herself fall asleep.

She dreamed a frightening, confusing dream about Emma Goldsbury giving away the secret of her shell game and then transforming into a giant grizzly that scared the crowd away.

Shelby startled awake. She sat up in her sleeping bag. It dark now, and cold. She was warm enough snuggled up in her bag, but outside it was cold enough to steal her breath away. She grabbed her headlamp from its spot near the tent's door. She pulled on the zipper to open the tent flap. In the quiet of the night, the zipper's whine sounded as loud as a scream. Shelby stopped pulling at it. She listened for movement inside nearby tents, hoping she hadn't wakened anyone.

The only sounds were Dad's snoring and the soft rustling of hemlock branches in the breeze. Even the bears seemed to be hibernating for the night.

She pulled on the zipper again, faster this time to get it over with. She was clumsy getting out of the tent and into her shoes. She turned on her headlamp and tiptoed across to Emma's tent.

Shelby looked around for the magician's backpack, careful not to shine the light on the nylon tent. No backpack outside. It must be in the tent. But Shelby had definitely seen Emma tuck something under the wood of her raised platform. That was what Shelby needed to find.

Shelby listened, perfectly still.

Emma breathed the steady breaths of deep sleep, her head inside the tent only inches from where Shelby needed to look.

Shelby squatted to see under the platform. She couldn't see anything. She leaned in closer for a better look and swung her headlamp around to light the corners. A couple of feet in, tucked up against the wall of the platform, was the zip-off pouch that matched Emma's pack. She reached for it, but it was out of her grasp. She stretched a little farther. Her fingers brushed it, but she couldn't grab it. One more time.

This time when she tried to grab the bag, Emma moaned and rustled just above her head.

Shelby froze. She quietly drew her hand toward her body. Her light shone at the ceiling of the platform, only a solid sheet of plywood separating her from Emma's tent.

"Who's there?" Emma whispered.

Shelby held her breath.

Surely Emma could hear her heart pounding. Shelby held still as long as she could. The way she was squatting and leaning over, though, it didn't take long before her legs started to cramp. She stretched one leg out behind her. Her toe brushed the ground.

Emma sat up. "I know you're there," she said.

A shuffling and some thunks told Shelby that Emma was about to get out of her tent.

Shelby pushed away from the platform and ran. Her first instinct was to run for her own tent, but she was afraid the noise would lead Emma right to her. She turned off her headlamp and headed away from her tent toward the woods. As soon as her feet hit the spongy moss of the forest, she squatted behind a log.

On the other side of the log, she heard footsteps approaching. A beam of light washed past. Shelby didn't move.

Emma swung her light back and forth a few more times. She walked a few paces and swung her light around again.

Shelby sunk down on the forest floor as quietly as she could. She waited forever and then waited a little longer. Emma's light went dark. The high whine of a tent zipper told Shelby the magician had given up looking and gone back to bed.

Shelby counted to a thousand before she moved back to her own tent. She tiptoed, careful not to make a sound. She climbed quietly back in her tent, but didn't zip it. The sound of the zipper would give her away. The crinkling of her sleeping bag sounded like thunder in her own ears. She hoped it would sound like all the other hikers tossing and turning in their sleep to Emma's ears.

She laid still and waited.

If she thought she was attuned to every little sound before, now it was amplified. Every twig snapping, every owl hooting, every camper turning over. She wasn't nearly as afraid of bears now as she was of Emma.

After a few minutes, a new sound started to bug her, the high whine of a mosquito right next to her ear. Shelby swatted it away.

It quieted for a few seconds before starting up again.

It had been a mistake to leave her tent flap open. Her warm body invited the insects in. An army of the flying beasts swarmed around her head. She brushed them off, but they came back for more. Their constant buzzing was enough to drive a girl insane.

Shelby dove inside her sleeping bag and cinched the cord tight around her head. Safe at last, she fell into a fitful sleep.

The sound of Cole thumping around on the platform woke Shelby in the morning. She opened her eyes. Or at least she tried to. Her left eye wouldn't open at all and the right one only opened a sliver.

She crawled out of her sleeping bag and scrambled out of the tent.

"What happened to you?" Cole asked. "Dad! Look at Shelby!"

Shelby held her hands to her face. Even without looking in the mirror, she knew she was swollen beyond recognition. Her face ached with oversized bumps. Her skin was stretched tight so it hurt to move her mouth.

Dad didn't offer much sympathy. "I saw your tent flap open this morning. You know better than that."

Well, she did now. "What do I do? How can I make the puffiness go down?"

"Time, cold, and maybe some antihistamine. Let me see what I've got in my pack."

"Should I use my EpiPen?" She always carried the shot with her in case she was stung by a bee. She was deathly allergic.

"Are you having any trouble breathing?" Dad asked.

She took in a deep breath and let it out. "No."

"Then you're fine. Just puffy. Hold on." While Dad hunted for some medicine to reduce the swelling, Shelby looked across at Emma. She didn't see the magician doing anything sneaky. But then, sleight of hand was her bread and butter.

Emma started up the path ahead of them. Shelby was disappointed that she hadn't figured out what Emma was up to. And she was embarrassed by her own stupidity in almost being caught. And especially embarrassed about being caught by the mosquitoes.

Emma might be ahead for now, but she had to sleep some time. They'd catch up with her tonight just like they did last night. This time, Shelby would be more careful. And she would *not* sleep with her tent unzipped, no matter what.

Chapter 9

Shelby couldn't do anything about trapping Emma until they caught up with her, and they weren't likely to catch up with her until they reached camp that night. So when Dad suggested they check out some ruins near Canyon City, she jumped at the chance. If she couldn't work on solving a case, at least she could do a little exploring. While Dad finished packing up their camp, she and Cole ran down a side trail. Rusted metal remnants from the gold rush days littered the ground near the river. A giant steam boiler rested like an abandoned submarine on the forest floor.

Cole kicked a rusty tin can deeper into the forest.

"Hey!" Shelby shouted. "Don't ruin the artifacts!"

"It's just garbage," he said.

"Yeah," Shelby said, "but it's really old garbage, so it's not garbage anymore." She found a rusty woodstove. Remembering the climb yesterday, she wondered how anyone had carried it so far into the woods. Did it used to have a house to go with it? Or did someone plan on taking it all the way to Canada and give up after the first day? She pulled on its handle, but the door was rusted shut.

Cole pulled off one of the burner lids on top.

A chipmunk squeaked at them from inside.

Shelby jumped, startled by the cheeky little creature.

It hopped to the edge of the stove. The ball of striped fur crouched on its hind legs and scolded Shelby.

"I didn't do it," she said, laughing. She pointed at Cole. "It was him."

Cole poked a stick into hole. The chipmunk jumped off the stove and scurried into the woods. "Hey, what's this?"

Shelby leaned in closer. "What's what?"

He pointed with his stick to something shiny hidden beneath the tangle of chipmunk nest.

Shelby reached in for it. It was a rock, shiny and yellow. "I think it's gold," she whispered.

Cole grabbed for it. "I saw it first."

But Shelby was taller. She grabbed it and held it out of his reach. "Just a minute."

The rock filled her palm. If all those people back in town got so excited over that tiny little gold coin, imagine how much a gold nugget as big as your fist must be worth. Thousands at least. Millions, maybe.

"Let's show it to Dad," Cole suggested. "He won't believe it."

A couple of kids finding a giant hunk of gold inside a stove in the middle of the woods? No one would believe it.

"What if it belongs to someone?" Shelby said.

Cole turned all the way around. "Like who? I bet it's been there ever since the gold rush. Maybe a miner hid it there. Maybe someone killed him for it."

"I don't know—" Shelby rubbed the gold.

"It's in the forest. Finders keepers, right?" Cole reached for the nugget, but Shelby pulled it back. "Hey! I found it!"

Shelby reluctantly handed it over. "Dad'll know what to do."

Cole took the gold and turned it over. It reflected in the light, but a cooler glow than the yellow of Emma's gold coin, probably because it was cloudier today. He stuck the rock in his hoodie pocket. "Just remember. I found it. It's mine."

Shelby stroked the vial with the flake of gold she kept tied around her neck. She wished she'd found one as big as Cole's. Or that she hadn't promised he could have the next gold they found. Her little fleck of gold looked silly in comparison. "I know."

All day long they climbed toward Sheep Camp. It wasn't a steep climb—that would happen tomorrow—but it went steadily uphill. Around noon, the gray sky let loose an endless supply of cold drizzle. Shelby dug through her pack for a rain jacket and waterproof pants. She didn't mind getting wet, but she didn't like

71

the idea of sleeping in wet clothes tonight. Her pack liner should keep everything dry.

They caught sight of one grizzly bear galumphing along on the hill opposite the trail. He wasn't close enough to pay them any attention, though Dad assured the kids the bear knew exactly where they were.

"Hey, Shelby?" Cole said. He kept his hands in his pocket. He was probably rubbing his gold nugget like some kind of lucky charm.

"Yeah?" she asked.

"What do you call a bear on a day like this?"

"I dunno. What?"

"A drizzly bear."

She groaned. She should have seen that one coming.

"What do you call a bear who's lost his dentures?" he asked.

"I give up."

"A gummy bear!"

It didn't get any worse than that.

"You know how to tell a black bear from a grizzly bear?"

Maybe it did get worse. "Dad already told us that one. It's the one with the bells, right?" Yuck.

"Nope." He turned and grinned at her. "If it chases you, climb the nearest tree. If it climbs the tree and eats you, it's a black bear. If it knocks the tree down and eats you, it's a grizzly."

Now even Dad groaned aloud.

Shelby shuddered. She did not want to get eaten by a bear of any kind. Ever.

Cole turned around long enough to point at Dad. "Gotcha!"

Shelby caught sight of her brother's pocket, weighted down by that giant gold nugget. Once she started thinking about it, she couldn't stop. She wished she saw it first.

She tried to think of something else, but the big gold rock kept pushing itself into her thoughts. She found herself trying to think of ways to get it away from Cole. This must be what they meant by gold fever. People would risk anything to get their hands on a little gold.

Shelby spent the gold a hundred times in her mind. She pictured pulling it out and drawing a crowd, like Emma had done. People would flock to her and beg her to share her wealth and knowledge.

When all Emma had was a coin and some cups, she did her act there in Skagway. But as soon as she made the gold, she'd packed up immediately and left town. Why? If she was really able to turn clay to gold, wouldn't she stay in Skagway and get as much clay as she could so she could make as much gold as she could? But she'd planned the hike a long time before, so the timing of turning clay to gold must have been on purpose.

Shelby needed to get closer to Emma if she wanted to figure out what the magician was hiding. Emma was already suspicious of everyone around her, but if Shelby kept her cool, a mosquito-bitten kid wasn't likely to draw suspicion.

Shelby ran through imaginary conversations in her head, trying to figure out what to say to draw Emma Goldsbury in.

"Can you teach me a card trick?" "How does your shell game work?" "I saw you performing in Skagway. You were amazing!" No matter how she imagined starting the conversation, Shelby couldn't figure out how to make it sound natural.

As it turned out, she didn't have to worry about it. When they got to Sheep Camp, Emma wasn't even there. Most of the others they had met at Canyon City had already arrived. A few others straggled in later. By dinnertime, only Emma was missing. Where had she gone? Surely she hadn't climbed up and over the summit already. She'd definitely left before them this morning and they hadn't passed her, so she had to either be here or farther along.

Cole went off to find firewood again. Dad worked on lighting the damp kindling. After several failed tries, he said, "We may have to hang out in the warming cabin tonight. I don't know if I can keep a fire going in this drizzle."

"I'll check it out," Shelby offered.

The warming shelters did draw a crowd. Ken and Kinsey had staked out their spot near the fire in one of the shelters. They wouldn't be allowed to sleep inside, but they'd stay in the warm, dry room for as long as possible.

No sign of Emma. Shelby wandered up the trail to a log cabin she'd spotted through the trees.

Ranger Robyn sat on an old rocking chair on the sheltered porch. When she saw Shelby, she stopped rocking. "Hey, I know you! What happened to your face?"

"Hi," Shelby said. "Mosquitoes."

"More likely no-see-ums. Yeah. I remember you. You were looking for that magician. Did you ever find her?"

"Yes, but I lost her again. Is she here?"

The ranger shook her head. "She was here earlier, but I don't know if she was planning to spend the night or hike on through. She'll probably be here tonight. She didn't get in early enough to make the summit by sundown."

"Isn't that super far?"

"Almost ten hours to the next camp."

The summit climb, the one she'd seen so many times in the old pictures, was the true test of determination. No way did Emma take on that much trail in one day. But where could she have gone? Surely she didn't leave the trail and try to make her own way through the wilderness.

"Thanks, anyway," Shelby said. If she hadn't hiked on, where could Emma have got to?

"Hey!" Ranger Robyn called after her.

Shelby turned around and looked at her through the brush. Maybe she had a suggestion where Emma might be. "Yeah?"

"You've got a permit, don't you? I'll be checking for them tonight. I'd hate to give you that ticket I was telling you about."

"Yeah. I've got one."

"No worries, then. I'll see you later."

Shelby trudged back to camp. Every trail had gone cold.

The magician had pulled her best disappearing act yet.

Chapter 10

So much for trying to strike up a conversation with Emma Goldsbury. Shelby couldn't even find her.

Shelby jammed her tent poles together and crammed them through the loops. She bent them to fill her tent with air, pitching it on the platform next to Dad and Cole's. She unstuffed her sleeping bag, and flicked it out harder than she needed to. It flew out of her hands. She grabbed it back to spread it on her camping mat.

Good enough.

She stuffed her backpack inside the tent and pulled the zipper closed. She did not plan to repeat last night's wrestling match with the mosquitoes. She grabbed her pack cover, her soggy socks, and boots. She could dry them in one of the warming shelters. When she climbed down off her platform, she took in the whole camp.

Emma's yellow tent was definitely missing.

She scanned the scene one more time. A flash of color against one of the platforms caught her eye. Could it be? She beelined over to it.

Emma's backpack. So she had been here after all. And by the looks of things, she intended to come back.

Shelby knelt beside the pack. More than anything, she wanted to unzip the main pocket and look inside. Just a peek. She was sure she would find the scale or the expensive electronic stuff Mom was missing from work. All she'd need was a few seconds.

She reached for the nearest zipper.

"Looking for something?"

Shelby jerked her hand back at the sound of Emma's voice. She looked up at the magician, feeling awkward and small and caught with her hand in the cookie jar. "No, I—" Shelby looked around for an excuse of what she was here. "I was picking up pinecones." She grabbed a couple that were beside Emma's pack. "For kindling."

"Pretty wet for kindling," Emma said. She reached a hand down to help Shelby stand. "What happened to your face?"

Shelby put a hand to her cheek. The swelling had gone down a lot since this morning, but she guessed she still looked like a puffy marshmallow or something. "Mosquito bites. I'm allergic." She backed up a little to give Emma more space.

"You should carry an EpiPen."

"I do, but Dad said if I can breathe, I'm okay." She took a deep breath to prove she didn't need a shot. "You know about EpiPens? Most people I meet don't have a clue."

"Sorta. I carry a pen for emergencies."

"What are you allergic to?"

"Nothing. I use another kind of pen, but it works the same way."

Emma leaned in and picked up her backpack. Before she did, she slid a small metal thermos into a side pocket. Shelby almost didn't see her do it, she was so quick.

Almost didn't. But she did see. The way Emma treated that thermos was the way she treated her cups in the shell game. Whatever Emma was hiding, Shelby bet it was inside that thermos.

Emma unhooked her tent from the top of her backpack.

"Need help?" Shelby asked. She didn't even give Emma a chance to answer before she took the opposite end of the tent and stretched it across the plywood platform.

Emma looked at her askance, but didn't say anything. Instead, she tossed her a pole to start assembling.

Shelby stretched the pole sections out and snapped them into place. She loved the way tent poles knew what shape they wanted to be.

Once the tent was up, Emma threw her whole pack over one shoulder and headed for a warming hut.

Shelby picked up her pack cover and followed. Whatever was in the thermos, she intended to keep it in sight until she had a chance to open it and see. Inside the warming shelter, she wouldn't have a chance to get her hands on it. Not with all those people circled around the fire.

Emma flopped her pack onto an empty bunk. She pulled a hat and some gloves out of a side pocket and hung them near all the others above the fire.

Shelby sat on a bench and untied her boots. She peeled her wet socks off one at a time. Her feet were white and squishy.

The conversation, which had abruptly halted when she and Emma came in, started up again.

"What else was stolen?" Steffan asked. He picked his teeth with a pocketknife.

Shelby's ears perked up. They were talking about the Skagway thefts.

Cole came in, letting in a blast of outdoor air with him.

"I heard it was all cheap stuff—clay, scales, a blowtorch. Some lead weights." That was Diane, a lady about Mom's age, but way thinner. She wore a wool sweater, matted down by the rain. They had met her the night before.

"There were some machines, too, right?" said Steffan.

"I think," Dad said with a twinkle in his eye, "it sounds like alchemy."

"What's alchemy?" Cole asked.

Shelby had heard that word somewhere before. Oh, yeah! Emma had used it in magic act. But what did it mean?

"It's when you turn lead into gold," Dad said.

Lead into gold? Was that why Emma stole all that lead?

"Whoa," Cole said. "You can really turn lead into gold?"

"Some people think so," Dad said. "All you need is some lead, of course, some basic lab equipment and tools for working with hot, melted metal. Oh, and the recipe, that's so top secret it might not even exist."

It was like the recipe for alchemy was the exact shopping list the thief had used. Dad might be right.

Shelby eyed Emma, looking for a reaction.

Emma stood in the ring of conversation but didn't speak. She made good eye contact with everyone. If she was guilty, wouldn't she do or say something that would let everyone know she was lying? Shelby wished she would look at the ground, or cross her arms, or walk away. But Emma didn't even flinch.

Shelby couldn't stand it anymore. She needed to force Emma to react. She stepped into the circle, pulled out a coin, and held it up. "Who wants to see me make this coin disappear?"

A couple of the older people kind of laughed at her in that "isn't she cute kind of way?"—the way you know they aren't taking you seriously. If they wanted to humor her, fine by her. She was more interested in getting Emma's attention.

She looked in Cole's direction and winked at him.

He winked back. Good.

"Watch closely, folks. I'm only going to show you once." She imagined her voice carrying like a carnival barker's, but it came out a little cracked. She held the coin in the air for everyone to see. "Does anyone have a handkerchief?"

She should have thought of the prop herself before she put herself in the center of attention, but it was too late now.

Kinsey whipped a bandana off the clothesline above the fire. "Will this do?"

"For sure." Shelby took the bandana with her free hand and covered the coin. "Come and feel that it's real," she said, holding the covered coin out for everyone to touch.

Steffan and then Kinsey stepped forward, reached under the bandana, and confirmed that, yes indeed, it was a real coin. Shelby gave Cole a nod that it was his turn. The trick would work better if it wasn't obvious he was her brother, but she didn't have another assistant lined up, so she'd have to take what she could get.

82

He reached under the bandana and felt the coin. "That's a real coin, all right!" he said loudly as if he were reading lines in a school play.

Shelby let go of the coin but kept her hand in the same position.

Cole took the coin and stuffed it in his pocket.

Shelby looked around to see if anyone had noticed. If they did, they weren't saying anything. Shelby spoke up. "Now I need you to help me say the magic words. Ready? One . . . two—"

On three, several people muttered a magic word. "Abracadabra!"

"Presto Chango!"

"Alakazam!"

"Voila!"

The mixture of all the magic words at once made everyone laugh.

Shelby pulled the bandana off her upraised hand and showed everyone her empty hand. "It's gone!" she said, hoping she didn't sound as surprised as she felt that the trick had actually worked. "Wait . . . wait . . . what's this?" She reached into her pocket and pulled out another coin, pretending it was the one she'd made disappear.

"And that's how you do it, folks!" she said, as if they were wondering.

"And that's a night for me, folks," Dad said. "I'm off to bed."

"Me, too," said Cole with an exaggerated yawn. Everyone else started gathering up their belongings and heading for their tents. "Ya coming, Shelby?"

Shelby knew she should get to sleep soon, but as long as Emma was still in here, Shelby would stay awake. "In a minute."

She pulled out her compass and fiddled with it while everyone cleared out. It was her most prized possession, a gift from Grumpa before she left on this trip. The glass was a little smudged. She polished it with the hem of her shirt.

"Nice compass," Emma said. She sat down on the bench next to Shelby.

"Yeah."

"I'll trade you." Emma reached into the air and produced a small, yellow rubber chicken.

"Agh!" Shelby jumped. Rubber chickens were creepy. "No thanks. You always carry chickens on you?"

"Among other things. Tools of the trade."

Shelby wasn't interested in pranks, just magic. She tucked the compass in her pocket and pulled out a coin. She didn't really want to talk about her compass with Emma. She rolled the coin across her knuckles. She was already getting better.

"Hey, good job on that trick tonight," Emma said. She tossed the chicken on the table. "I could show you a better way to do it if you want."

"Seriously?" After all her plotting on how to spend more time with Emma, Shelby never expected it to fall into her lap.

"Yeah. I always like to help young girls who are interested in magic. The famous magicians are all men, but I plan to change that. Maybe we could hike together tomorrow?"

"Cool," Shelby said. She couldn't believe it. "That'd be great."

"I hope you have several coins to practice with."

"Enough," said Shelby.

If she weren't so exhausted from lack of sleep the night before, Shelby wouldn't have slept at all. She kept playing through different ways she would trap Emma into confessing. Finally, her imagination slowed and she fell into a deep sleep in which she dreamed about handing the Illusive Emma Goldsbury over to the police.

They rewarded her with bags of gold.

Chapter 11

Shelby rubbed her hands together to warm them, but nothing would thaw her frozen fingers. She'd been shivering since Dad had awakened her and Cole at five this morning.

"Rise and shine, lazy heads!" he shouted into their tents. "An early start means an early summit!"

An early start was fine, but this early? Shelby snuggled down in her sleeping bag for just another minute or two. The gentle patter of rain lulled her back into her dream.

"Out of bed!" Dad called. "Hot water's ready. It's an oatmeal kind of day!"

Shelby moaned and sat up. She stretched. Her hand hit the tent wall, sending the droplets that clung to the roof of the orange fabric tumbling like a little river to the ground outside. Still in her sleeping bag, she wiggled into the jeans she had kept close to her through the night to keep them warm. When she crawled out of the bag and the tent, the morning's cold bit at her. How could it be so freezing in the middle of the summer?

Dad thrust a mug of oatmeal at her. She clutched it with both hands. Within a couple of minutes, all the heat had gone out of the metal mug.

After a quick visit to the camp outhouse, Shelby looked around for Emma. She was eager to cash in on the offer of hiking together and talking magic.

"Come on, slowpokes," Dad called. "Most of the others have gone."

He was right. Almost everyone had cleared out before Shelby pulled herself out of bed. She looked across to Emma's platform.

Her tent was gone, and so was her backpack. Shelby couldn't believe she hadn't waited.

Cole wiped his eyes with the backs of his gloved hands. "Can't we go back to bed? I'm sleepy."

"Not today, Champ," Dad said. "Today we go to Canada."

Shelby quickly packed her tent in its bag and bungeed it to her backpack. The quicker they got ready, the faster they would catch up with Emma. Even if she had to sprint, Shelby planned to overtake her. She wondered how long ago Emma had left.

Shelby hiked her heavy pack onto her back. She was sore, but she felt stronger today than she had at the beginning of the Chilkoot. "Come on, guys. Let's get going." She looked toward the trail. "We've got to hurry."

Dad laughed. "We've got plenty of time to make it over the summit. Slow and steady . . ."

Slow and steady was great for climbing Long Hill and the Chilkoot Pass, but it would never get her caught up to Emma.

Cole threw on his pack and bolted past her to the trail. "Last one there is bear bait!"

Shelby took off after him.

"Bear bait is right! Stay in sight!" Dad called.

Not far up the path, they met Emma heading back toward Sheep Camp. Her eyes met Shelby's then darted away. She slid past them.

Shelby turned and watched Emma run back to camp. She started after her.

"Where do you think you're going?" Dad asked.

Shelby stopped for a second. "Emma said we could hike together today. I need to make sure she knows I'm waiting for her. Just a minute."

Dad gave her a puzzled look, then waved her on. "We'll wait here for you. Hurry."

Shelby ran back to camp, careful to let the forest's undergrowth hide her from Emma's line of sight.

The magician knelt beside the wooden sleeping platform where she had spent the night. She reached for something hidden beneath the boards. Whatever it was, Emma stuffed it into her backpack. She looked up to see if anyone had seen her.

Shelby ducked.

So the magician *was* hiding something. But how could Shelby get anyone to believe her? They already thought she was just a nosey kid who wanted to pick on a lady trying to make an honest living at her street performance. Only Emma wasn't an honest lady. Whatever was in that little bag could help Shelby prove it.

Emma slid her pack onto her back. She started straight toward where Shelby was hiding.

Shelby ran up the path, hopefully before Emma could see her through the underbrush. "Come on, guys. Let's go!" she called as she passed Dad and Cole. She wanted to be well down the trail before Emma came their way.

Once they were far enough ahead, Shelby slowed way down. She dragged her feet along the trail. Every time she did, Dad called out, "Hurry up. Slowpoke!"

At the bottom of Long Hill, Emma finally caught up.

Shelby picked up her pace to match Emma's.

"I'm ready to learn that trick," Shelby said.

"Oh, yeah." Emma seemed distracted.

Dad turned around. "Are you two going to stick together?"

Shelby looked at Emma, hoping she'd say yes.

"Sure," Emma said with a shrug.

Yes!

"I'm going to move a little faster for Cole. Okay?" Dad asked.

"Sure," Emma said.

Shelby couldn't believe he would leave her to walk alone with a practical stranger, much less one that was sure to prove to be a bad guy. It was the best thing that had happened all day.

"We'll let you two get to know each other. We'll wait for you at the bottom of the Scales."

"Scales?" Shelby pictured the stolen scales from the museum back in Skagway. And she pictured Emma's golden plate.

"The Scales is the name of the hard climb on the way up to the Chilkoot Pass," Dad said. "Like in the picture of the gold miners."

"Ah." She'd seen a hundred old photos of a long line of men climbing a snowy slope up to the Canadian border. "Great! We'll see you there."

Emma and Shelby hiked behind the guys. As soon as they were out of earshot, Emma said, "You brought your coins?"

Shelby dug in her pocket. Where were they? They must have fallen out.

"Never mind," Emma said. "I've got one here." She pulled a coin out of thin air and tossed it to Shelby. "Let's see what you've got."

Shelby caught the coin with both hands. She held it between her thumb and finger, flipped her hand like she'd seen Emma do, and dropped the coin on the path. She picked it up and tried again, but it was much harder to disappear a coin when you're walking than when you're standing still.

Emma grabbed it from her. "It's all in the wrist. Watch." She didn't slow down, but made the coin vanish as she walked. She reached to the sky and pulled it out of the air.

"How'd you do that?" Shelby asked.

Emma tossed the coin back to her. "A magician never tells," she said.

Shelby was disappointed. Why offer to show her magic if she wasn't going to tell the trick?

Emma laughed. "Ha! Just kidding. You should see the look on your face!" She showed Shelby her technique and then told her to practice. "You have to do it over and over and over again until it becomes second nature. It's like the coin is a part of you that you can control like your fingers or toes."

Shelby was so focused on the coin, she snagged her boot on a tree root. She put her hands up to catch herself. Soft fir needles cushioned her fall. She brushed her hands on her jeans.

"Don't look at the coin," Emma said, reaching down to help her up, "or you'll never get it right. Look at what you're doing, where you're going, and the trick will come into focus for you."

Shelby thought about Emma's advice as she worked on the trick. Maybe looking for whatever Emma was hiding was the same way. If she looked at it straight on, it would never be clear, but if she focused on something else, she'd see it clearly without even needing to think about it.

Chapter 12

Emma and Shelby walked single file for a long time. Shelby kept practicing moving the coin through her fingers, careful to look down every couple of seconds to watch for rocks and roots. The trail moved always uphill. The thick evergreen forest thinned and shortened. They were approaching the tree line, the elevation above which no trees would grow.

She wanted to ask about the thefts without drawing attention to the fact she thought Emma was responsible for them. She rolled the words around in her head as she rolled the coin around her knuckles.

"Hey, Emma?" she said.

"Yeah?"

"Did you hear about the stuff that was stolen in Skagway before we left?"

Emma was quiet for a long time. Finally, she said, "No. Why?"

"No reason," Shelby said. "Just some weird stuff taken is all."

"I didn't hear anything." Her eye twitched, but was that because she was lying or because a mosquito landed on her?

Shelby was hoping for more of a reaction. Probing more now would be too obvious, and possibly unsafe, since she and Emma were alone. She'd try to bring it up again later.

Above the tree line, they entered a rocky valley. The trail took them ever upward. Then, in a field of boulders, it became no trail at all.

"How do you know which way to go?" Shelby asked.

Emma looked back at her. "As long as we're moving up, we are going the right way. See?" She pointed ahead to a range of mountains. "The lowest point up there is our summit. Once we round that point, it's all downhill."

The rain had mostly stopped, but clouds still hung low over the mountain ridge. To Shelby, the summit looked impossibly far. And way, way up there.

They met Dad and Cole sitting on a huge rock near where the mountain steepened.

Cole was gnawing on a hunk of jerky.

"You want to climb with us?" Dad asked.

Shelby looked at Emma. She still needed time with her. She had more questions, but needed to build up the courage to ask them. "You guys go on ahead. We'll be all right."

Cole scurried up the first boulder.

Shelby looked up the mountain. It didn't look like the pictures she'd seen at all. "Where's the snow, Dad? I thought we'd be climbing in the snow."

He shook his head. "The gold miners did the pass in the winter. It was easier, believe it or not. You get to do it the hard way." He took off after Cole, turning back to yell, "Lean forward into the rocks. Don't let your pack pull you backwards. Remember you've got the extra weight on your back. We'll see you at the top."

This was no simple uphill hike. It was an enormous maze in which the object was to always step up without getting stuck atop a boulder that was a dead end. Several times Shelby found herself on a rock that led to no other rocks. Either the way forward was up another boulder too tall to climb or it was down into a hole. Whenever she hit a dead end, she had to turn around and scoot down on her bottom. She couldn't see where her feet were going to land, so she felt around with her toes, looking for a solid spot to step on.

Dad and Cole were way up the hill. Emma was just ahead of her. Shelby tried not to look too far ahead. It was enough to focus on the rocks right in front of her.

She scrambled up a monstrous rock. She thought she could step from it across to the next one, but once she got to the edge, she realized it was too far to jump. She would have to climb down and find a different route.

"Jump. It's not too far!" Emma shouted.

Shelby looked up at her. Emma was watching her.

Shelby looked at the next rock. No way could she jump that far, even without a pack on.

"You can make it!" Emma shouted.

Shelby wasn't sure her legs were long enough. But Emma had made it and she wasn't much taller than Shelby. She could do it. She stood on the edge of the boulder and judged the distance to the next rock. She took a couple of steps back and counted: "One, two, three!"

She lunged off the edge.

One foot landed solidly on the edge of the boulder she was aiming for. The other fell a little short.

She leaned forward and reached her hands out. Her pack was too heavy. It dragged her backwards.

Her right foot slipped from the rock. She clawed at the boulder. There was nothing to grip.

She slid between the two boulders. It felt like she was falling, falling, falling.

Suddenly, she jerked to a stop. Her pack stuck between the rocks. She was wedged there. Her feet dangled above the ground. She'd only fallen a couple of feet.

Immediately, fear turned to embarrassment. She wiggled to get herself free, but she couldn't reach the ground below or the ledge above.

She felt like an upside-down turtle.

"Help!" she yelled.

"Whoa, kiddo." Emma dropped her pack and scrambled down to her. She shucked off her backpack and reached out her hand.

Shelby grabbed it.

An electric shock shot through her body. A buzzing rang in her ears.

"Whoops, sorry." Emma pulled her hand away. She twisted a ring off her finger and stuck it in her pocket. "My handshake buzzer. I forgot I was wearing it. Try again."

This time when Shelby grabbed her hand, there was no shock or sound. There was also no budging.

Shelby was stuck fast.

Chapter 13

B y the time Dad made his way back down the boulder slope to where she was wedged between the rocks, Shelby had slipped enough that the two boulders squeezed the air out of her.

She tried not to panic. If she started struggling for breath, she might slip even farther and get squooshed even more. Or worse, she might fall and break a bone 15 miles of hard hiking from ether end of the trail.

Cole stood above her and squinted.

Dad got right down on her level, practically laying on the rock beside her so he could look her in the eyes. "Are you hurt anywhere?"

She shook her head. "I don't think so." She took another shallow breath. "But it's hard to breathe."

"Stay still for a minute while we figure this out. As long as you're not bleeding anywhere, I'd like to keep it that way. I am going to try to pick you straight up. Okay?"

She nodded. She wished he'd hurry.

Dad looked at the others. "Cole, Emma, when I get her up far enough, help her feet get a hold, okay?"

They both scrambled to get on either side of her while Dad positioned himself right over her.

"Ready?" Dad bent his knees and hooked his hands in her armpits. "One . . . two . . . three." He pulled and grunted and moaned.

Shelby didn't budge.

Cole scrambled into the hole below her. From down there, he could push his body against her legs. "Try again, Dad!" he called.

Even with Cole pushing and Dad pulling, Shelby was super stuck.

Dad sat down next to her and scratched his head. "Plan B," he said.

"There's a plan B?" Shelby wiggled her feet to make sure her toes were there.

"There will be."

"We could cut her backpack straps," Cole suggested. "Maybe then we could pull her out without the pack."

Dad considered it. "It might work. Does anyone have a pocketknife handy? Mine is uphill where I dropped my gear."

Shelby did. She always carried whatever tools she might need. "My Leatherman's in the top pocket on my pack."

Emma tugged on the top on the pack. "I'll get it."

Shelby heard the zipper open and then close.

Dad took the knife and opened it. "You've got the sawblade on here?" he asked.

"Yeah, somewhere."

"Got it," he said. He started sawing her straps. "One down," he said. "How you doin'?"

She wiggled her feet again. At least she still had feeling in them. "Okay, I guess. Are you almost done?"

"Just a sec."

She felt his hands moving near her left shoulder as he worked on the second strap.

"Okay, done."

Dad got in position above her, Cole below. On three, Dad pulled on her armpits.

This time she moved a little. "You almost got it!" she cried. "Try again!"

This time, when they pushed and pulled, the backpack fell down and Shelby shot up. She scrambled to get her feet beneath her on top of the rock. She gave Dad a big hug, Emma a high five, and Cole, still down in the hole, a low five.

Cole handed her pack up to her.

Dad had butchered the straps. She thought he'd cut straight across at the seams, but he had hacked at them every which way.

"How am I supposed to carry this?" Shelby asked. It was hard enough climbing without having her arms full of backpack.

Dad picked it up. "I'll attach it to mine for now and carry it the rest of the day. We can work on repairing it at camp tonight."

"Lucky," Cole said.

She *was* lucky, she thought.

While Dad strapped her pack to his with bungee cords, she watched Emma climb ahead of them. Cole pulled his chunk of gold out and tossed it in the air, caught it and put it back in his pocket.

It might be his gold, but the reward would be all hers.

Climbing was much, much easier without her pack. Shelby scrambled to the summit ahead of all the others. She waited for them so they could snap a selfie standing in the U.S. and Canada at the same time. Shelby watched Emma to see if she looked more pleased than the rest to have left the U.S., but everyone was grinning so much and congratulating themselves and each other, it was hard to tell. She seemed happy, but so did everyone.

They started down the slope. It was easier than climbing, of course, though Dad walked slower than normal under the weight of two packs.

They descended through the snow above a giant blue lake. The white slope swept down from where they walked and slid beneath the deep blue water at lake's edge. It looked to Shelby like if she lost her footing, she would slide down, down, down into the freezing water below. She paid special attention to where she planted each step.

At last, weary and hungry, they arrived at Happy Camp, barely more than a wide spot in the trail. In the warming cabin a sign read "Happy Camp. Where happiness goes to die."

Shelby flopped down on a log by the path. "My feet are killing me."

Cole glared at her. "Imagine how you'd feel if you'd had to carry your own pack."

Shelby glared back. It wasn't her fault.

"Hey, lazy bones," Dad said. He dropped Shelby's pack by her feet. "No resting yet. You've got to pitch your tent, fix your dinner, and help me get this pack fixed. I'm not carrying it tomorrow."

She dragged herself to her feet. Pitching the tent was easy.

Next she walked down to the stream to get some water. She ran it through her filter and brought it to a boil. The water went in a foil bag and turned into lasagna. At home, she would *not* eat something so smushy. Hikers can't be choosers, though, and she was starving.

She finished every bite, even licking the inside of the foil.

Now all she had to do was fix her pack and she'd be free to investigate.

She and her dad sat near the campfire and looked at the straps together. "Do you think we could just duct tape it?" Shelby loved a good duct tape repair.

Dad turned one of the straps over in his hand. "I don't think so sweetheart. We're going to need to do a proper repair job if you're going to hike with this thing on your back for two more days. You've got a sewing kit, right?"

Of course, she did. She had everything in her pack. She ran to get it out of her tent.

"And your pocketknife and some paracord," Dad called after her.

Sewing kit. Check.

Pocketknife. Check.

Paracord. Check.

She would take her small bundle of duct tape, just in case. She reached in and rummaged around, but didn't see it. She reached her hand in the pocket and dug through it. First aid kit, EpiPen, emergency blanket. She finally found the duct tape in the bag with her mirror and compass.

Only her compass wasn't there.

Where was Grumpa's compass?

She pulled everything out of the pocket and looked through it. No compass.

No way had she put it in another pocket. She might misplace something like a wad of tape, but she would never misplace her most prized possession. She tore through the other pockets looking for it.

"Dad?" she called. "Have you seen my compass?"

"The one your Grumpa gave you? No."

She backed out of the tent. "It's missing."

"Are you sure? Maybe you stuck it in your pocket."

She hadn't. It should be inside the bag with the mirror and other emergency supplies.

"It's not there." She stuffed her hands in her jeans pockets, as if it would suddenly appear there.

"Where did you last see it?"

In her backpack, of course. Before that? She tried to think. "I had it at Sheep Camp last night. I was trying to see which direction we would take to get to the pass. I showed it to Emma there, then I put it away. I didn't get into that emergency bag since then." She talked faster and louder. "It was there, I swear."

"Calm down," Dad said. "Let's think this through."

He helped her lay out everything from her pack, but they didn't find it. He suggested they talk to the other campers. Maybe someone had seen it and picked it up for them. Or maybe they could call Ranger Robyn once they reached civilization to see if she had seen anything back at Sheep Camp.

She was sure she'd put it in her bag. There was no way she'd left it behind. She had closed it carefully inside the bag with the mirror in it and put the bag in the top pocket of her backpack, just like always.

She hadn't been in that pocket since.

But Emma had. It was the same pocket Emma had opened to get a pocketknife to cut her straps.

Aha!

"Emma took it," Shelby blurted. "She pretended she was helping me and she stole it."

"Whoa, Hon. You're jumping to conclusions."

"No, I'm not. She took it. It's the only explanation." Shelby started for the warming hut with purposeful strides.

"Where are you going?" Dad called after her.

"To find Emma and get my compass back."

She heard him coming behind her. "Stop, Shel. You can't just accuse someone of stealing without any proof. Shelby, slow down."

She had proof enough. It all added up. Emma had the means—her ability to use her fingers to play tricks; she had the motive—her obsession with golden things, and she had the opportunity. Shelby burst through the door of the warming hut. A dozen or so people sat around a table. Emma and Cole were among them.

Shelby pointed at Emma. "She stole my compass."

Every head in the place turned to Emma.

Emma looked up and squinted at her, her eyes gray as steel. "What compass?"

"The one I showed you. The one my Grumpa gave me. The one you said you wished you had." Now everyone was looking at Shelby.

"I don't know what you're talking about. You never showed me a compass."

"Did so. Back at Sheep Camp." She looked at the group around the table. She caught a couple of pained expressions. "I did too show it to her."

Emma shrugged. "She's a kid. Who you gonna believe?"

"Her," Cole piped up, pointing at Emma. "She doesn't lie."

She was pretty sure she heard him whisper "anymore" very, very quietly. She stared at the magician, watching her every move. Emma was a sneaky one, but Shelby was onto her.

She narrowed her eyes at Emma.

Emma glared back at her, unblinking.

And then, for a tiny fraction of a second, Emma's gaze darted to the corner of the room and then back again. It was so quick, Shelby almost didn't notice. But she *did* notice. She looked toward where Emma had glanced.

The magician's backpack stood propped in the corner. Not her huge hiking pack, but the smaller one that could zip off and be a smaller bag. Shelby's compass must be inside.

Shelby lunged for it. Before anyone could stop her, she unzipped it and dumped its contents onto the table.

"Aha!" she shouted, fully expecting her compass to be on the top of the stack. Instead, there was a small thermos and a bundle of syringes held together with a red rubber band. Another bag held a bunch of injector pens, just like the EpiPens she carried in her own backpack, only a little bigger and silver. What in the world? Shelby looked at Emma.

"I'm diabetic," Emma said. She lifted the hem of her shirt just enough to show a little black device attached to a wire that led to a circular patch on her stomach. "That's my insulin. Without it, I would die."

"But," Shelby sputtered, "you were acting weird and hiding it."

"Not hiding it—keeping it safe and making sure it stays cool."

"But—"

"Look, I don't like to talk about it. It's awkward, okay?"

Shelby's face turned hot. She felt a hand on her shoulder and heard Dad say, "You've done enough, Shelby. Time for bed."

He led her out of the warming hut like she was a little girl. She hung her head, embarrassed to have made a fool of herself in front of everyone. She never should have dumped out Emma's bag.

She knew Emma had taken her compass, as sure as she knew she'd stolen the stuff in Skagway. But now she'd made a fool of herself trying to prove it. Even if she did come up with the proof, they'd never believe her now.

Chapter 14

Shelby hardly slept that night. Despite a hard day's hike, she couldn't get what happened in the warming hut out of her mind.

Her compass was missing. That was a fact.

Emma had swindled the people in Skagway. That was a fact.

Emma had stolen stuff from Skagway to pull off her trick. Shelby couldn't prove that yet, but she knew it was also fact.

Emma was trying to hide something last night, and it wasn't the fact she was diabetic. After all, she'd already told Shelby she took shots using a pen like the EpiPen. So, that wasn't the secret. It was something, though.

She wanted to get into that bag again, but there was no way Emma—or anyone else on the hike—would let her anywhere close to it. If she had dumped the bag and all the stolen goods, including her own compass had fallen out, then she would have had a case. As it was, no one was going to believe her if she accused Emma of anything again.

The next day's hike, easier in the sense that it was mostly downhill, was somehow more difficult for Shelby. Dad was still cross with her and Cole just shrugged when she tried complaining to him. She obviously couldn't hang out with Emma anymore and all the other hikers seemed to be avoiding her, too— maybe afraid she would rip into one of their backpacks or announce to everyone that they were, in fact, the thief, not Emma.

She ran the evidence over and over, and every way she thought about it, she came up with the same conclusion. Emma Goldsbury had swindled those people in Skagway. She had stolen the things she needed to do it. And she had stolen Shelby's compass. But how could she prove it? And why would anyone believe her?

She'd tried cozying up to Emma. That hadn't worked. She'd tried rifling through her bag, but hadn't found anything. She'd tried accusing her outright, which had completely backfired.

So now what?

Mid-morning, they hiked down below tree level. The forest on this side of the mountains was much drier than on the Alaska side. Shelby dragged her feet along the rocky trail, kicking up a cloud of dust that sent Cole hacking and kept Dad in front of her. There were still plenty of lakes and even snow left on the mountain slopes, but the mossy undergrowth she'd grown accustomed to was missing and under the spindly trees lay sparse dry plant growth and a lot of dusty gravel.

They reached Lindeman Lake in the early afternoon. The campground here was built on a flat area along the lake's edge. A sign said that during the gold rush, thousands of tents used to crowd the shores. Shelby couldn't imagine that many people living in this empty wilderness. From here, she could only see a half a dozen tents. Emma's was pitched on the far end of the campground. A few more might arrive later, but what used to be a busy city was now just a stopover for through hikers.

She had to do all her camp setup, but first, she had to find a toilet, and fast. She ran for the pit toilet. Outhouse buildings were always gross, but it was better than going in the woods. She pulled on the handle of the little wooden building.

"Occupied!" called someone from inside.

She'd know that voice anywhere. It was Emma.

Shelby thought about walking away, but she really had to go. Really, really. She would just ignore Emma when she came out, same as she was sure Emma was going to do to her. There was no reason they had to talk to each other or even make eye contact.

When Emma came out, she shot a surprised look at Shelby, then lowered her gaze and skirted around her.

110

Shelby bolted past her and locked herself inside the outhouse. She used the toilet as quick as she could, then waited as long as she could to give Emma plenty of time to disappear. It smelled terrible in here. She held her breath. When she couldn't stand it any longer, she unbolted the door and pushed through it into the sweet fresh air.

Emma waited, arms crossed, in the middle of the path.

"Excuse me," Shelby said. She kept her head down. She didn't want to talk to Emma, didn't want to see her.

Emma stood her ground.

Shelby tilted one way and then the other, looking for an easy way to walk around the magician, but devil's club lined the path on both sides of the trail. She'd already had a run-in with the thorny plant. As far as she was concerned, in any fight with devil's club, you end up the loser.

She cleared her throat and repeated, "Excuse me? Can I get by?"

Emma glared at her. "What's your problem?"

"I—I can't get past you." She knew that wasn't what she meant.

"What's your problem with me? What have I done to you? You keep following me, watching me, and now accusing me of stealing your thing."

"My compass. Why did you say you'd never seen it before?"

"Why did you say I stole it?"

"Because you did. You're the only one besides my dad and my brother who even knew about it."

"What if it wasn't stolen at all? What if it fell out of your pack when I was helping you?"

Shelby hadn't thought about that possibility. She'd been so sure it was zipped in the bag, she hadn't considered it could have been loose in the pocket and just fallen out. "I guess—" No, that wasn't right. It was in the bag. It couldn't have fallen out.

"Right. You guess right." Emma sneered. "Just keep your nose out of my business and your fingers out of my pack. Got it?"

Shelby nodded. She didn't even want to talk to her, much less bother her anymore.

"Perfect. Have a nice rest of your hike." Emma waved her past as she stepped back far enough for Shelby to get around her.

Shelby could have sworn she saw the flash of something golden in Emma's hand as she waved . . . her compass!

She lunged for Emma and caught her off balance. She knocked her to the ground. "Give me back my compass!" she yelled.

"Get off me!" Emma kicked and rolled, struggling to get out from under Shelby.

Shelby reached for Emma's hand. She *had* to get that compass back. "Give it here!"

Emma pushed her off without much effort. Shelby landed on her bottom in the dirt. Emma wasn't that much bigger than her, but she was surprisingly strong. Emma was already getting to her feet.

Shelby stood and went to tackle her again.

Dad's voice came from right behind her. "Again, Shelby? What's going on with you?"

Shelby turned to see him. He was beyond disappointed this time. He looked super angry. And it took a lot to get Dad angry. She pointed at Emma. "She's got my compass. I saw it!"

Dad shook his head. "I'm so sorry," he said to Emma.

Emma smiled in a way that adults tend to believe, even though Shelby knew it was completely fake. "I don't know what she thinks she saw. Maybe it was this?" She turned her right hand over to reveal a golden dollar in her palm. "I carry this all the time. It helps me keep my fingers nimble."

"That's not what I saw," Shelby blurted. "It was bigger and not as shiny." She knew what she saw. Her eyes were *not* playing tricks on her, even if Emma was.

"Shelby," Dad said, using his "we're not going to discuss this now" voice.

"It's not," she said, putting in the last word even though she knew it wouldn't make any difference.

"Again, I'm sorry," Dad said to Emma. How dare he side with a total stranger over his own daughter?

Emma took off in one direction and Dad steered Shelby in another. When they got far enough away from the toilet that he could scold her without being heard, he laid into her with a "leave Emma alone" this and a "keep your nose out of it" that.

"I know what I saw," she said. "She's got my compass. And a bunch of other stuff."

"You are not to speak to that poor woman again on this hike. Leave her alone. I don't know what she's done to you to make you so hostile, but it's ridiculous. Let her finish the hike in peace."

On the outside, Shelby said the words, "Yes, sir," but on the inside, she was screaming, "Why don't you believe me?" She knew the answer. It was because she'd told a few white lies recently that led to bigger lies that ended up getting her and Cole into a pretty dangerous situation. She had not earned Dad's trust back yet.

"Just leave her alone or I'll staple you to me for the rest of the trip."

He would, too. Dad was great at coming up with clever and embarrassing punishments. She wouldn't put it past him to literally duct tape her to him for the duration of the hike.

"Okay," she muttered.

"And you need to apologize."

Oh, no way. She might be able to avoid Emma, but that was no way she was saying sorry to that low-down, snake-bellied—

"Not right now, but before the hike it over. Deal?"

Shelby moaned. "Can I think about it?"

"Tomorrow's the last day of the hike, so think fast."

She rolled her eyes. "Can I go now?"

"Go where?"

Anywhere away from camp. Anything to get out of this conversation. She pointed up the hill.

Dad thought about it for a minute. "Take Cole with you. And be back in time for dinner.

"Do I have to?" She didn't want to invite Cole along. She just wanted to be alone.

"Yes. For your safety."

She crossed her arms and stomped away. She'd be fine without Cole, just for a few minutes.

"And Shelby?" Dad called after her. "I love you!"

She just kept walking.

Chapter 15

Shelby stomped off in the direction of the hill. She couldn't believe Dad was siding with Emma. Again.

She'd seen the compass. It wasn't a trick of the eye. And it wasn't a golden dollar. But right now Dad wasn't believing anything she said. She didn't want to care about whether Emma was the robber or not, but she couldn't help it. There is was, right in front of her, and she couldn't make anyone believe her.

She pushed through the trees up the path to the top of the hill. More than anything, she wanted things to be all right with Dad again. He was disappointed in her and she couldn't stand the feeling. But what could she do to win back his trust?

For one thing, she could stop accusing Emma of stuff to her face. That didn't seem to work well.

Other than that, she knew it would take time to heal over the lies she'd told in Juneau. She wished there were a faster way.

She broke out of the trees into a clearing. On the edge of the clearing were some fenced-in rectangles. If she didn't know better, she'd say they were graves.

She walked over to one of them. A wooden cross stood on one end of the rectangle. It marked the grave of a man who had died along the trail during the rush to the Klondike. Hard to imagine people being so crazy for gold that they would risk their lives for it.

Unbidden, the memory of holding the hand-hewn gold coin Emma had produced out of clay flashed in Shelby's mind. It was so bright, so soft. Maybe it wasn't so strange. Gold made people do crazy stuff.

She turned away from the grave. It wasn't worth it. No one should have to give up their life for a chunk of metal. She would apologize to Emma. Then everything would be right with Dad again. That's what was worth being stupid about—family. She wished she had her compass back, but at least she'd only lost the compass, not Grumpa who'd given it to her. She missed him like crazy.

From the other side of the hill, she heard a cry.

Cole!

She was supposed to keep him with her. How could she be so careless?

"Help!" he called again. That was Cole all right, but he sounded kinda squeaky. He was in trouble.

Without thinking, she ran toward his voice. Across the clearing and down another path, she followed the sound of his cries, one after another, yelling for

117

someone to help him. "Coming!" she called back, as loudly as she could. "Hold on, Cole. I'll be there soon!"

She found him at the base of the hill.

His feet were planted in place, his back to her, his palms down.

In front of him, not 20 feet away, a bear stared back.

Shelby stopped in her tracks.

The bear stared at her, its beady eyes fixed on hers. Its head was massive. Its grizzled hair stood up in spikes around its face.

Shelby stared back, frozen. She was close enough to see the moisture on the bear's nose.

Everything Dad had taught them about bears fell out of her brain. "What are we supposed to do?" she whispered, loudly, to Cole.

He reached back and grabbed her hand. "I was hoping you would know."

All she could remember was that someone said getting killed by a bear doesn't hurt.

She didn't want to find out if they were right or not.

"Just stay calm. And don't look him in the eye," she said. She shifted her gaze to follow her own advice.

"What if it's not a him?" Cole asked. "What if it's a mama with cubs?"

Shelby pulled gently on his hand to start backing him up. She could hear the bear's snuffling breath above the beating of her own heart. She wanted to turn and run, but didn't want to turn her back on the beast. "I came from behind you. I didn't see any cubs." She talked out loud now, remembering that making noise helped the bear know you were there. This bear, obviously, knew they were here. They were standing right in front of it.

Cole took a step back with her.

The bear took a step forward. It grunted. Its breath smelled of rotten fish.

"Make yourself look big," Shelby hissed. Some of Dad's advice was coming back to her. She threw her arms in the air.

Cole put his arms up too.

The bear cocked its head to the side. It looked more curious than scared.

Shelby and Cole stepped back again.

The bear didn't move.

They could probably run. They'd probably be okay. But probably wasn't good enough odds. Shelby wouldn't turn unless she knew for sure.

Suddenly, a metal clanging echoed across the hill. It was coming from behind, getting louder and louder.

A woman yelled, "Git! Scat! Shoo!"

The bear moaned, low and long.

Shelby's knees trembled.

"Go on, now! Git!" the woman yelled.

The bear turned and waddled into the bushes.

Shelby yanked on Cole's hand, dragging him away from the bear. Not far behind them stood Emma Goldsbury, clanging two brass plates together and yelling at the top of her lungs.

"Th-thank you," Shelby stammered.

"Don't mention it," Emma said. Her words sounded strong, but her face was white. She trembled and let the plates clatter to the ground.

"Are you okay?" Shelby asked.

Emma nodded, but she didn't look so good. Probably because she was so scared of bears. "I heard him screaming and ran to help."

Cole mumbled, "I wasn't screaming," even though he had been. Shelby would have screamed, too, if she had been alone.

Emma did that for Cole ever though she was terrified of bears. Shelby owed her something. It was time to quit trying to prove she was the thief, even if she was. "Truce?" Shelby asked. She wouldn't accuse Emma of anything ever again. She didn't have to save them, but she did. "I'm sorry."

"Truce," Emma said, reaching to shake Shelby's hand.

Chapter 16

Shelby helped Cole stuff his sleeping bag into the bottom pocket of his backpack. Since their bear encounter last night, she hadn't let him out of her sight. Nothing like staring into the teeth of death to remind you what's important in life. She didn't even feel much jealousy when she caught a glimpse of the gold nugget amongst his stuff.

Cole was most definitely important.

Annoying? Sure. But he was her only brother and she intended to keep him alive. She'd even sidled up to Dad at the picnic table last night and offered to play three thirteen, which he loved. She felt better after she apologized to Emma who, even if she was a thief, had saved their lives. That outweighed her faults.

She never did prove anything about Emma and now she never would. She wouldn't even try. If her suspicions were correct, Emma would keep heading farther into Canada when the rest of them hitched rides or rode the train back to Skagway. Her disappearing into the wild would kind of prove it, she guessed, but then it would be too late. She pushed thoughts of the reward aside.

"Ready?" she asked Cole. She had, as usual, double-checked her own pack before strapping it on. Everything was in place. All zippers closed. All emergency supplies in easy reach. All strings tucked in. Everything but her missing compass.

Cole's pack, by contrast, looked like a squirrel's nest. Strings hung out all over the place and he'd zipped his dirty clothes pocket in a way that one of his socks was stuck in the zipper teeth. Mom would be thrilled.

"Ready!" He hoisted his pack on with a grin and grabbed his walking stick.

Shelby's own pack was still holding together, but it would need a proper repair job once they got back to town. It wouldn't hold forever.

"Let's go, then!"

Dad said today would be a shorter hike and there would be a hot meal of moose burgers and apple pie at the end of the trail. She wasn't too sure about the moose, but apple pie made a lot of things worthwhile. So she hadn't caught the thief or earned the reward. At least she'd hiked the Chilkoot.

The morning sped by. They caught some great views of Lake Bennett, their ultimate goal, which made Shelby move all the faster. With the end in sight, she and Cole raced for the finish, moving ahead of Dad with his approval as long as they promised to stay together.

Less than a mile from trail's end, Shelby noticed a group of hikers blocking the path. She thought it strange, since most of the hikers had walked alone or with only one or two other people the whole way. The first thing that came to mind was that it was another bear. She slowed down. She didn't want to meet another one so soon.

Cole ran ahead of her.

The sound of frantic voices reached her before she reached them. Most of the people who had stayed at Lindeman last night were gathered in a semi-circle. Someone was lying on the ground.

Shelby pushed between elbows to see who it was.

Emma.

She was pale as a snowfield, and covered in a sheen of sweat despite the fact it was a cool, overcast day. She was breathing shallow and twitching, like she was having a seizure.

"What happened?" Shelby asked.

Kent spoke up. "She was fine and then all of a sudden she was talking nonsense and before we knew it, she was on the ground."

"She's diabetic," Shelby said.

"That's right," Kinsey said. "But what do we do about it?"

Shelby reached automatically for the smaller of Emma's packs which lay on the ground just outside the circle, the one she'd dumped out in front of everyone back at Happy Camp. The insulin was in here. When she unzipped the bag, all the different stuff fell out. There were so many choices of needles and liquids, she didn't know which to grab. "Which one?"

The adults all just stared at her. No diabetics in the group, apparently.

Shelby grabbed for the ones that looked like her EpiPen. Emma said they worked the same way. She hoped she was right. Shelby pulled the cap off with her teeth. There was no needle.

"I need a needle," she said. "Quick!"

Someone scrambled for the bag. "Which kind?"

She didn't know. "Something that fits on the end of a pen." She didn't remember seeing anything like that in what had fallen out of the bag. "Check the thermos."

After a second, but what seemed like forever, Cole cried, "Got it!"

They passed the thermos through to Shelby. She untwisted the cap and looked inside. Several needle tips were nestled against one side. Those would do. She pulled them out to use.

Something in the bottom of thermos caught her eye. Under the bundle of needles, glinting in the light, was Grumpa's compass.

Chapter 17

Unbelievable. The compass was in the bottom of Emma's thermos.

Emma *had* stolen it.

Shelby didn't have time to think about that now. If she didn't get this shot in Emma, and fast, the magician might be making her final curtain call. Shelby reached for a needle and tossed the thermos aside.

She quickly attached the needle tip onto the pen. She twisted it and held the pen in her fist. She hoped she was doing the right thing. With as much courage as she could muster, she jabbed the needle into Emma's thigh.

Everyone got perfectly quiet.

Shelby held the pen in Emma's leg. She counted to ten like she'd been taught to do with her own pen. If it didn't work, she didn't know what to do next.

She pulled the needle out. She held her breath and watched Emma for any changes.

For the longest time, nothing. Even Emma's twitching stopped. It didn't look like she was breathing.

Shelby sat back on her heels. She'd killed her. Her heart grew inside her chest, squeezing her lungs.

"Wake up," she muttered. "Come on, Emma. Wake up."

She looked around at all the adults. No one was breathing. They were all just staring at Emma.

"Come on, Em," Shelby prayed.

Emma's eyes fluttered open.

Shelby closed her own eyes and let out a huge breath of relief. She hadn't killed her after all.

"Hey!" shouted Steffan. "She's awake!"

Someone clapped Shelby on the back. "She's awake! You saved her!"

Emma blinked. She pushed herself up on one elbow. She swayed.

"Whoa, now," Ken said. "Take it easy for a minute. You don't want to get up too fast."

Shelby didn't even watch to see what happened next. Now that Emma was awake, she wanted to get as far away as she could, as fast as she could. She felt a tangle of emotions, happy Emma was going to be okay, but deeply hurt that she'd lied so many times and so well.

Shelby leaned over and picked up the small thermos. Her compass still sat in the bottom. Holding the needles to one side, she tipped the compass out

126

into her hand. She looked around. No one was paying any attention to her. She slid the compass into her pocket.

It was the proof she'd been looking for. She could wave it around and show everyone she was right all along. But she didn't feel like it anymore.

She glanced back at Emma.

She was sitting up, but still very pale. Ken and Kinsey stood between them so Shelby couldn't see her.

There was nothing else they could do for her. Shelby tipped her head toward the trail and said, "Come on, Cole. Let's go."

Chapter 18

Shelby dug her fork into the pointed end of her slice of apple pie. She eased the bite to her mouth and let the sweetness sink into her tongue and melt down her throat. It was the best thing she'd ever tasted. Well, second best after the moose burger she'd just polished off. Who knew moose could taste so good?

Cole shoveled his pie into his face at an alarming rate.

"Good, right?" Shelby asked, taking another careful bite.

"Reawy ummy," he said, his cheeks stuffed with pie.

Dad walked over with his own plate and sat at the picnic table next to Cole. They'd opted to eat outside the restaurant since, after four days on the trail, they smelled too ripe to be in the company of the regular diners.

"Well, you did it," he said. "You hiked the whole thing. Congratulations. How do you feel?"

"Awesome!" Cole announced. "Let's do it again."

"Wish we could, Sport. What about you, Shel?"

Shelby thought about it. Her feet ached, sure, and her shoulders were a little raw where the pack straps had dug into them. Other than that, she felt great about finishing the hike. So why the twinge of disappointment? "Good, I guess."

"You guess?"

She reached in her pocket and pulled out her compass. She set it on the table between her and Dad.

"Where'd you find that?" he asked. "Was it in your bag all this time?"

She shook her head. "Emma's bag."

"Now, Shelby—" His voice turned stern. "We've talked about this."

She hurried to explain herself. "In her thermos. When I was looking for her needles."

"Why didn't you say anything?" His face flashed a mix of pride and bewilderment.

"It wasn't the right time. It was more important to help her live than to make sure everyone knew I was right."

"And after?"

"I kind of stopped being mad at her and started being sad for her. Besides, I got my compass back."

Steffan, Ken, and Kinsey came over to the table, plates loaded high with pie. "Can we join you?"

"Sure." Cole and Shelby scooted over to make room.

"Did you hear?" Steffan said.

"Hear what?"

"Your daughter was right all along. We helped Emma make it to the end of the trail. I was putting her needles back in her pack when I saw some of the stolen stuff"

Shelby stopped chewing. Her eyes opened wide. There was more in the pack than the compass. Of course there was.

"Whadcha find?" Cole asked.

"A couple pieces of electronics, the brass scales, and this." He pulled out a cell phone and found a picture.

Shelby looked at it first. It was the cover of a book or pamphlet of some kind. It read Metal Clay Magic. "What is this?" she asked. Where had she heard those words before? She tried to remember.

They sounded like a whisper. Of course! The gypsy woman in Skagway.

Kinsey spoke up. "It's this special clay you can buy. It looks like normal clay, but it's got real gold in it. When you heat it up, the clay burns away and leaves you with the gold. Expensive, but very effective."

Which was how Emma had turned the clay into gold. And got all those people to give her money.

Metal clay magic.

"Oh, and this." Ken swiped his phone to advance to another picture.

Shelby whistled. "That's a lot of money."

"Over seventy thousand," Ken said. "Another reason to sneak across the border. I knew it all along.

"You—" Shelby couldn't believe he was saying that. He and all the others had refused to believe her.

Emma was the next to reach the outdoor eating area, but she wasn't alone. She was escorted by a tall police officer.

"What about all those other people?" Cole said. "I mean, if she really stole all that money like we think she did, shouldn't we try to help them get their money back? If she stole my gold nugget, I'd want it back, even if you already got your compass."

"What gold nugget?"

Shelby and Cole turned to see the policeman right behind them. His badge read "Royal Canadian Mounted Police."

Cole shrunk down in his seat.

Suddenly, Shelby was glad the gold didn't belong to her.

"Can I see it?" The Mountie didn't seem angry, but he wasn't joking either.

Cole got the gold out of the side pocket of his pack. Reluctantly, he handed it over to the lawman. "I found it fair and square. I didn't steal it, I swear. I was gonna show someone, but there was a thief on the trail, so I didn't want to—"

The Mountie interrupted him with a raised hand and a smile. "You didn't do anything wrong, son. At least nothing against the law. Hope you're not planning to pay for college or buy a new car with this rock, though."

Cole took it back. It flashed bright when he turned it at a certain angle. "Why not?"

"What you've got there is a nice chunk of fool's gold."

"Fool's gold? Really? It looks real."

Shelby asked, "How can you tell?"

He leaned in close to the rock. "See how it's got sharp corners on it? Gold is more rounded. Besides, real gold catches the light at every angle, not just from one direction. Once you've gotten to know the real thing, there's no substitute."

Shelby couldn't believe it. She thought she'd known the real thing and she was sure this was it. She reached to her necklace with the tiny gold flake inside. It wasn't much, but at least it was real.

Dad walked back over. "So, you'll be taking her in?"

"Yes, sir. Looks like we have enough evidence to try her in Canada and the U.S. It'll be up to the courts to decide which country gets her first. Theft and fraud. Thanks for your help, kids." He reached out his hand.

Shelby shook it.

He had a strong grip.

"We should go," Dad said. "The train leaves soon."

Cole stuffed his gold rock back in his pack, hefted the bag onto his shoulders, and raced for the train. "All aboard!" he called and ran for the train.

Shelby picked up her patchwork backpack. She reached for her compass on the table. It felt comfortable in the palm of her hand. She might have made a fool of herself, but at least she'd done it for what she knew was right.

Shelby glanced behind her to where Emma sat at a table, her hands cuffed behind her back. She wasn't mad anymore, just sad that such a talented magician had chosen to use her gift to steal and deceive. She hoped getting caught would start Emma heading the right way.

The train let out two loud whistle blasts.

She started toward it, but the Mountie's voice stopped her.

"One more thing," he said.

She turned to face him. "Yes, sir?"

"There's a nice reward waiting for you in Skagway. I hear you're the one to thank for catching our crook."

A grin spread across Shelby's face. She was getting credit *and* she was getting the reward. Not bad for her first day in Canada. "Yes, sir. Thank you, sir."

"Better run. Your ride's about to leave without you."

The train slowly started rolling down the tracks. Shelby ran to catch it. She grabbed the handle and pulled herself onto the platform between cars.

She turned and waved at the Mountie who smiled and waved back.

Before stepping into the train car, she looked ahead at the tracks. Somewhere out there, her next adventure was waiting.

Author's Note

Shelby and Cole are the same age my brother and I were the first time we hiked the 33-mile Chilkoot Trail. It was a magical trip, climbing the Scales from Alaska into Canada, knowing we were climbing over the same rocks the prospectors did in the great Gold Rush of 1898.

Most of the men and women who made their way over the Chilkoot and into the Klondike did not find their fortune. The ones who got rich were the ones who sold supplies to the miners, who offered goods and services, and those who (like Soapy Smith) swindled the hopeful miners out of what little they brought with them.

If you ever get a chance to hike the Chilkoot Trail, or any other long trail that takes you far into the wilderness, I highly recommend it. Just be sure to watch for bears!

Stay tuned for Shelby and Cole's next adventure, this time in the Yukon.

Patty Wyatt Slack

About the Author

Patty Wyatt Slack was born and raised in Juneau, Alaska. She grew up tromping the trails of the Mendenhall Valley, beachcombing up and down Lynn Canal, and fishing glacier ice out of a glacier lake for making homemade ice cream.

She now makes her home slightly farther south, but still in the Northwest, with her husband, their daughters, and a dog named Marble. Every time she gets a chance, you can find her hiking in the woods.

If you ever hike the Chilkoot, maybe you'll meet her there!

Want to go on more adventures with Shelby and Cole?

Be sure to read their first adventure, *True North*.

And then pick up the Drake kids' third adventure, *Midnight Run!*

For other books by Patty Wyatt Slack, visit pattyslack.com